What the critics are saying...

Magick Men: A Shot of Magick

5 *Stars!* "If you like your hero super alpha with attitude, sarcasm, and a sexy as hell growl, you will definitely find him right here." ~ *Faith Jacobs Just Erotic Romance Reviews*

5 *Stars!* "Definitely a keeper on my shelf, Rhyannon Byrd is on the fast track to becoming one of my favorite authors." ~ *Angel Brewer Just Erotic Romance Reviews*

5 *Flames* "I hope there will be a long series of the Magick Men books to come. A very EXCELLENT enjoyable book to read!" ~ *Sharon Sizzling Romances*

Once Upon a Midnight Blue

"...There is passion, desire, deep emotion and intrigue in this story. The heat is at an all-time high..." ~*Robin Taylor, In the library reviews*

"... proves to be another perfect example of why Ms. Walker is quickly becoming a name to be reckoned with in erotic romance." ~*Mireya Orsini, The Road to Romance*

"Another great edition in the Not-So-Grimm Fairy Tale series...an erotic short story from the up-and-coming Shiloh Walker that is not to be missed!" ~*Courtney Bowden, Romance Reviews Today*

Spell of the Chameleon

MORE THAN MAGICK

Rhyannon Byrd,
Titania Ladley
&
Shiloh Walker

More Than Magick
An Ellora's Cave Publication, February 2005

Ellora's Cave Publishing, Inc.
1337 Commerce Drive, Suite 13
Stow, Ohio 44224

ISBN # 1419951661

Other available formats: ISBN MS Reader (LIT), Adobe (PDF), Rocketbook (RB), Mobipocket (PRC) & HTML

Edited by: *Briana St. James, Pamela Campbell*
Cover art by: *Syneca*

Warning:

The following material contains graphic sexual content meant for mature readers. *More Than Magick* has been rated *E-rotic* by a minimum of three independent reviewers.

Ellora's Cave Publishing offers three levels of Romantica™ reading entertainment: S (S-ensuous), E (E-rotic), and X (X-treme).

S-*ensuous* love scenes are explicit and leave nothing to the imagination.

E-*rotic* love scenes are explicit, leave nothing to the imagination, and are high in volume per the overall word count. In addition, some E-rated titles might contain fantasy material that some readers find objectionable, such as bondage, submission, same sex encounters, forced seductions, etc. E-rated titles are the most graphic titles we carry; it is common, for instance, for an author to use words such as "fucking", "cock", "pussy", etc., within their work of literature.

X-*treme* titles differ from E-rated titles only in plot premise and storyline execution. Unlike E-rated titles, stories designated with the letter X tend to contain controversial subject matter not for the faint of heart.

CONTENTS

Magick Men: A Shot Of Magick

By Rhyannon Byrd

Chapter One

Lachlan McKendrick awoke in an agony of sensation—his tall, powerful body shuddering with the lingering memories of mind-blowing sex.

He had dreamt of her again last night.

Not one of those fleeting dreams, like the whisper of a butterfly's wings that hovered at the nebulous edges of your consciousness. No, this had been a white-hot, raging blast of physical sensation that had tormented him the whole night through, scraping down his nerve endings like a vicious force of nature.

She'd come to him in brutal, sweet visions of flesh, lust and need—an angel from hell who had tortured his senses—and last night had been particularly painful.

No sooner than his eyes had closed, his cock already hard from thinking of her, had he heard her husky voice whispering in his ear, the sound ethereal and far away, although her breath was sweetly erotic against his hot skin.

"Is this for me?" she'd drawled, her slender hand wrapping around the wide base of his cock, not afraid to grip him with a strong, tight pull as she'd milked the long length, wringing rough shouts of pleasure from his throat. He'd bucked beneath her, his big hands biting into her flesh, desperate to keep her where he could fuck her to his heart's content.

Her fingers had tightened, her thumb stroking across the broad head of his aching cock, smearing the salty moisture streaming there from the slit, driving him insane. "You're a witch," he'd gritted through his clenched teeth, the guttural words being torn from his soul. "And if you're not careful, I'm going to be fucking you like one."

She'd given a throaty laugh, moving against him in a delicious press of flesh against flesh, and he'd felt the slippery sweet cream spilling from her cunt, dripping down the insides of her strong, lean thighs as she'd wrapped herself around him.

"You don't scare me," she'd murmured thickly. Her tongue had licked a line of fire from his ear to his collar bone, taking gentle nips from his warm flesh, her wicked hands holding tight to his throbbing cock. "Do with me as you dare, Magic Man. I can take you. All that you ache for—whatever you need—I want to be the one who gives it to you."

The seductive words had cut loose his tenuous control and he'd eagerly swallowed down her sharp gasp of surprise as his mouth had taken ownership of her own. His tongue invading like a sword, he had deftly flipped her beneath him.

"Now!" she'd cried into his mouth, her nimble tongue tangling with his, her desperation just as needy, just as violent in its quest for satisfaction. She'd spread her legs wide, lifting her hips, trying to take the too long, too thick mass of his cock within her hungry pussy, but he hadn't been ready to ease her ache so soon.

Ignoring her snarling groan of frustration and pulling hands, Lach had licked his way down her shivering length, feasting upon the taste of need riding her so high. He loved that he was the only man who could make her burn. The only one who could make her scream her pleasure. She didn't need to tell him he was the first lover who'd made her come—her pleading body told him all he needed to know.

He'd sucked gently at the soft skin just above her sexy little patch of blonde curls, the honey swirls of hair already glistening with the juices creaming from her delectable, sopping cunt, assaulting his senses. "Oh shit," he'd heard her moan, and he couldn't help but smile against her fevered skin. She was such a pleasure; one he longed to gorge himself on over and over in an eternity of forevers.

His hands had held her silky thighs spread wide as he'd shifted to look down at her. His nostrils flared as he'd devoured the beauty of her drenched flesh. He'd never known a woman who appealed to him more, as if she'd been made just for him, from the demure pink lips, wet with cream, to the tight bud of her clit, berry red and ripe to bursting. And the tiny hole he loved best of all. The intoxicating taste, like warm melted sugar and strawberries. The way it gasped like a little mouth, aching to be ripped open—fucked till she shouted and screamed and writhed in the throes of ecstasy. The way cream spilled as he had lapped it into frenzy and then had dribbled down his throat with the first plunge of his tongue as it dug deep inside.

He had teased her, eating at the pulsing flesh until she'd pulled his hair, shouting, "Now, damn it! I said now!"

"Such a bloodthirsty little bitch," he'd laughed, covering her trembling body with his own. He'd nestled the huge round head of his cock within the sweet, cream-covered lips, pinned her grasping hands high above her head, and taken her as hard as he dared, knowing in his dreams he could not harm her.

He'd pounded—slammed her with his cock, forcing himself through the delicious clench of her tight pussy, nudging her womb. He'd ridden her writhing body with all his power, reaching between them to spread the puffy sweet lips of her cunt farther apart, holding them wide, wanting her to feel every inch—every slide of his engorged penis. Over and over he'd buried himself to the root, cramming her full of cock till she was blood red and gasping, the rhythmic clenching of her pussy pulling feral, beastly sounds from his throat.

The orgasm had gathered in the roots of his soul, blazing through his blood, scorching and urgent and full as he'd ground against her soft womanly body, praying for the release he knew would never come.

It never did.

And last night was no different.

He had woken up alone and aching. His throbbing cock standing tall and angry, furious at fate for teasing him with a taste of the one woman he couldn't have.

"Fuck!" he'd roared through the silence of his room, throwing off the sweat-soaked sheets that had still smelled of her cream and grabbing the nearest clothes he could find.

At six-five, he was tall and mean and muscle-honed from all the long, grueling hours he spent training other *Magicks*—Warlocks and Witches—in the arts of combat and self-defense. He had thick, reddish-brown hair that he normally kept trimmed much shorter than his outrageous cousins, light green eyes, and golden skin. He was well-dressed, always in control of his strong, passionate emotions, and wealthy enough to afford any luxury he wanted, from houses to cars to women. Though sex was one thing he'd never had to pay for.

He'd always had a look of danger, but now that look took on a more sinister character. His hair was longer, shaggy around the strong bones of his face, jaw dark with auburn stubble, big body wrapped up in ragged jeans, a black T-shirt, and big black boots as he left his house to pace the early, fog-filled streets of Edinburgh.

He looked like the kind of man you wouldn't want to meet in a dark alley, and he felt like one as well. And to be honest, he didn't know how much more of this he could take.

You'll take as much as you have to, man, his Warrior's pride warned. *Because you canna let those blasted fools win. Not this time! You've pledged them your bloody loyalty, but they havenna any claim on your cock!*

Yeah, well, too bad the governing High Council of Magicks—made up of his five outrageous uncles—thought otherwise.

They'd put a bloody curse on him, the well-meaning fools. One that changed his women into fucking animals every time he shot his blasted load. And the only way around it was to find his *bith-bhuan gra*—his soul mate.

His uncles, it seemed, had taken it upon themselves to ensure that he stopped sowing wild oats and began planting a few instead.

In the belly of the right woman, of course.

It was intolerable. He was so full of sexual frustration his skin felt like it was about to burst. Hot, tight, and disturbingly prickly, like an itch beneath the surface that remained just beyond his reach. He'd tried alleviating the painful pressure on his balls himself, taking matters into his own big hands, but ended up putting his fist through his shower wall when he'd been unable to bring release.

That was apparently yet another one of the Council's twisted concoctions. According to their sadistic curse, he could only achieve an orgasm with a woman. And if he didn't want to find himself shooting his cursed load of magic in front of another friggin' furry pet, he had to find the true woman—whatever the hell that meant.

It means we're royally fucked, man, his pride chimed in again. *Completely screwed.*

"Shut up, will you," he growled, wondering when he'd become crazy enough to argue with himself.

The Council Leader, his Uncle Seamus, wasn't seeing him or taking his calls, which left him to rely on his cousin Kieran for information.

There wasn't much. And looking back on it, Lach could only thank Saephus he hadn't actually been inside any of the five Witches he'd bedded, or *Cailleachs* as his people called them, at the time of release or he'd probably be sentenced to death right now for assassinating his elders. So far there'd been a cat, a monkey, a goat, then a goddamn smelly sheep (he was Scottish, but he wasn't *that* bloody Scottish), and finally a foaming at the mouth Rottweiler. That particular occasion had turned out even worse than those before it. Becca was a big enough bitch on the best of days, and it'd cost him a tetanus shot and five stitches for the fucking bite she'd put in his leg.

Because the wound had been made by another *Magick*, he hadn't been able to use his own power to heal it.

And the dreams, well, they were their own kind of torture.

The whole situation was ludicrous, especially for one as powerful as he. Why not Kieran or Dugan, Mal or Blu? One of his wild cousins who would laugh it off and go with the flow, or at least not kill themselves thrashing against it.

And to make matters worse, he was beginning to believe there wasn't enough magic in the world to save him.

"If there was," he snarled beneath his breath, "I'd have bloody found it by now. I'd be fucking myself blue, instead o' wasting my time lusting after a woman I canna have!"

He'd been walking the barren streets of the city for hours now, searching for answers, huddled within a black leather jacket, the biting cold of the wind stinging against his face as it whipped around his head. And yet, a part of him—a part he didn't want to admit was there—knew he was waiting for the hour of seven to roll around once again. Then he'd find himself standing in the doorway of The Wicked Brew, his eyes hungry for just a glimpse of the one thing that brought him even a glimmer of peace these days.

He'd found *her* three weeks ago, when he was on a walk just like this one. And he'd dreamed of her each night since.

There was only one problem.

Well, one on top of the fact that his uncles had plagued him with a freaking curse on his cock and he couldn't screw without shooting a load of magic that turned his women into angry animals, leaving them craving a piece of his ass to chew on.

His balls were blue, his time was running out, and instead of searching for the true *Cailleach*—his *bith-bhuan gra*—he'd become obsessed with *her*. She was goddamn fascinating, beautiful and intelligent and spirited as hell. So different from any woman he'd ever known before.

There was just that one minor, somewhat unfortunate detail.

The woman who haunted his sleep and every waking hour was not a *Magick*.

She was not of his kind.

No, the woman of his dreams was a fucking mortal.

Chapter Two

Lach stood before the door of the café undecided, longing to go in every bit as much as he wanted to run like hell in the opposite direction. It was an internal struggle mired in lust and fear and the strange need to protect the little mortal from a power that was far too dangerous to risk her with.

And, of course, he couldn't discount the unfathomable fact that he was unequivocally scared shitless of her.

He didn't understand it, this bizarre effect she had on him.

The only thing he did know with any degree of certainty was that if he'd had his way, he'd have fucked her at that first intoxicating smile, regardless of the obstacles. And there were plenty. His family, this infuriating curse, and that whole mortal thing.

He didn't do mortals.

At least he never had before. His power was formidable to most *Magicks*, his size and strength overwhelming to even the strongest of the *Cailleachs*.

But to a human?

Well, he'd always known he could be damn near deadly.

So he'd never traveled down that particular sexual road before, and to be honest, he'd never really cared to.

Until now.

But he couldn't do it. Only Saephus knew what the load of magic erupting from his cock these days would do to a human mortal if he tried to fuck her.

And the worst part of all was that she wanted him too. She wanted to be ridden just like in his dreams, crammed so full of cock she could barely breathe.

The first time he had ever set eyes on her he'd known. He'd smelled her erotic scent, seen it in the heat of her eyes and the sensual curve of her lips the moment they first came face to face. He'd been out prowling the early morning streets when he'd wandered into the quirky shop and found her standing behind the counter, laughing with another customer. He'd been longing for some relief from this continual nightmare, his leg burning with stitches and his cock on the verge of implosion, and there she was.

It'd been an instantaneous reaction, from the physical surge of his pulse to the emotional clenching of his heart. Something inside of him had recognized her on every level as a man, and he'd been back every goddamn day since.

Yeah, his pride grumbled. Because you canna stay away.

She'd become an addiction, and at this point, despite the incessant need for her ripping at his insides, she was the only thing that gave him a moment of calm. He was hooked, craving that warm feeling of belonging she invoked in him like a junkie hungered for his fix.

All he had to do was see her and it was as if a shroud of contentment fell over him. Something steady and comforting, like home. And yet, at the same time it was as volatile and raging as the molten belly of a volcano, twisting him with physical need.

It was fucking pathetic. Here he was, the most powerful of the *Magicks*, and he'd been reduced to hovering on the doorstep of a mortal café, afraid of entering the world of the *gnach* because of one puny little female.

"Fuck this," he growled beneath his breath, shaking off the dramatic musings of his over-exhausted mind. He may not have figured out a way around the fucking curse, but he could sure as hell handle a woman.

With that thought in mind, Lach squared his shoulders and walked inside, hoping to inconspicuously disappear into a dark corner, but for a man of his size and bearing, not to mention his rugged good looks, it was impossible to go unnoticed.

He hadn't taken two steps past the threshold before she looked up at him, smiled her siren smile, and murmured, "Hey, Magic Man."

She'd called him that from the first, though he wasn't sure why. There was no way in hell she could know what he really was, or how true a nickname she'd chosen.

Despite his resolve to remain unaffected, the mortal's smile hit him like a flash of heat spilling through his cold bones, beating against the rhythm of his heart.

Without warning he had a sudden flashback to one of his dreams. "Mmm," she'd drawled, her wicked tongue taking hungry licks of his throbbing flesh. "I love your taste, your shape, your size. You've a beautiful cock, Lachlan McKendrick, and I want it to belong to me, as does your heart."

Then she'd stuffed her mouth full of him, swallowing down his shaft till he could swear he'd hit the back of her throat. But it wasn't just the amount of cock she could swallow when so many women could barely take half of a man his size. No, it was the way she sucked at him so greedily, as if she took as much pleasure as he did, her pink tongue rooting into the slit, always eager for his taste.

And the little hum in the back of her throat drove him wild. He fantasized about what it'd be like to be able to fill that humming little mouth full of scalding come. To feel her cheeks and tongue and throat working as she swallowed him down with greedy satisfaction.

Saephus, it'd be so good it'd probably kill him.

"What can I get ya?" she asked, ripping him back to the present, and his cock demanded he answer, "*You*."

He only just managed to resist the dangerous impulse. Or better yet, push her to her knees, pull out his monstrous hard-on, and let her show him just how much she loved swallowing. Instead, he mumbled, "Colombian. Black. No sugar," and stalked off to the corner table by the window.

He faced the street, trying to ignore the shudder of need her husky voice sent through him each and every damn time she spoke to him. Of course, he was no more successful today than at any other time over the last three weeks. His cock grew long and hard and thick within the confines of his jeans, and he wondered for the thousandth time how he was going to survive never having this woman beneath him, her legs spread wide, delectable cunt open—wet and aching, just waiting for him to fuck the shit out of her.

The image was so clear in his mind he could almost taste the juices spilling sweetly over his tongue, sliding down his throat, filling his belly. Behind him, she gave a throaty laugh at his usual cranky reply and there was an answering twitch in his jeans, his cock insistent in its demand for satisfaction.

"Goddamn traitorous body part," he grumbled beneath his breath, knowing the fucking thing was going to be the death of him. She set his steaming cup before him, making his head spin as her teasing feminine scent hit him hard, assaulting his already bruised senses.

Against his will, he looked up at her reflection in the window, the hazy picture in no way diminishing the impact of her face and figure on his aching body. She was beautiful, yes, but he'd had beautiful women before and they'd never had this kind of effect on him.

Women were a pleasant pastime, a necessary recreation meant to be enjoyed and then set aside for the next in line. They were not—*not*—meant to be hungered for. They were not things that he *needed*. And they sure as hell weren't the objects of his obsession.

Except for this one.

Her figure was firm, yet seductively lithe. Not particularly tall, but then neither was she short. She was, in the most mundane of phrases, the perfect height, and with all the right curves in between. Then there was the blushing golden skin—which he knew would go raging red when she creamed for him—hair the color gold of a good whiskey, and those damn eyes. Ice gray, ringed with a deeper charcoal, framed by fine arched brows and thick lashes. And when they looked directly at you, it felt like a fucking lick of fire down your spine.

It was a burn he couldn't get out from under his skin.

She held his stare in the window, waiting it seemed, as if expecting—or maybe hoping for something from him, but finally relented with another lift of her lips and walked back to her station behind the counter, resuming her work as if they hadn't just filled the steamy interior of the café with enough physical heat to warm the whole blasted city. The answering twist of his gut drew the lines of his scowl deeper, so that he looked on the verge of a thunderous rage when Kieran found him but a moment later.

His cousin stood beside the small table, his own irritated expression revealing his personal frustrations. "If you're not going to answer your fucking phone, Cousin, then why in Saephus' name did you give me the blasted number in the first place?"

Lach took a slow sip of coffee, watching beneath his brows as Kieran angrily crammed his big body into the seat across from him. "Maybe because I havenna felt like talking?"

Kieran's look was deep and direct. "And if I'd had something important to say?"

He snorted. "Then you'd have known how to find me, which is exactly what you've done. Now, isn't it?"

Black hair flowed over broad shoulders as Kieran shook his head. "Och, but you havenna made it easy, Lach. It's times like this I wonder why I even bother with you." But they knew it was a lie. They'd been the best of friends their entire lives; either would have gladly given their blood for the other. Though these days, Lach wasn't sure just how much his blood was worth anymore. Taking another needed shot of caffeine, he decided to get the bad news over and done with.

"Your meeting with the almighty Council last night?" he drawled, his deep voice thick with sarcasm. "Were you able to discover anything new from our esteemed elders?"

This time it was Kieran's turn to give a snort of disgust as he slouched back against the gleaming wood of the chair, his big hands slapping against the surface of the table. "Those miserable old fools won't relent, Lach. Not even my father would budge on the issue. I talked myself blue and they still won't give a fucking inch. The curse stays until we find a way around it."

A growl of frustration rumbled from Lach's throat, the infuriating news combined with the mortal's intoxicating nearness pushing him to the limits of his fraying control.

"Fuck! Do they think I'm going to just keel over to their harebrained schemes and let them dictate my life? Do those stubborn idiots even understand what they're dealing with here?"

The grooves around his mouth and at the corners of his eyes grew deeper, the exhausting effort it took to control himself clearly taking its toll. He looked bleak, angry and dangerous, like a man who'd reached his limit and would soon have nothing left to lose.

He stared into the steaming darkness of his coffee, his big fingers tight around the thick white mug in his hand. "I don't know how much more of this I can tolerate, Kieran. This miserable fucking mess is going to push me too far, and then we're all going to pay for their meddling."

And it wasn't just the not screwing part that was driving him crazy. No, it was the fact that he wasn't screwing the little mortal working behind him. Her image remained powerfully clear in his mind even when he wasn't looking at her, as if it'd been burned into his subconscious for an eternity of torture.

"They're nearing the end," Kieran murmured, studying him out of eyes that were far too dark and wise for his slightly younger years. "I know you're pissed, and you have a good right to be, but what they've done, they've done outta love. They want to see the family secured, the McKendrick line assured for the future, and you're the oldest power."

Lach was too furious to listen to excuses and diplomacy, his emotions strung too tight. "And will you be so gracious when your own turn comes?" he snarled, his eyes glowing red, raging and ready for a fight.

Kieran's mouth twisted with dark humor. "So long as they dinna try to mate me with something that has more legs than I do—and more hair, I'll try."

The glow softened, but a slow burn still smoldered in the light green depths of his Warlock eyes. "So you say now, but it'll be interesting to see what happens when it's your own life they're pulling the strings on."

"And you'll be there to enjoy my misery, won't you?"

The corner of Lach's mouth kicked up in a reluctant, answering grin. "Smiling like a jackass," he muttered beneath his breath.

Kieran's rough laugh burst out over the gentle noise of the café, and Lach watched in the window's reflection as the mortal looked over to their table, her gaze curious—and as always, as hungry as his own. She walked to him, one hand holding a carafe to refill his cup, but he knew it was only a ruse. He could smell her need for him in the coffee-scented air, strong and pure, and knew he was scenting just as heavily. They were like two beasts in heat, just waiting to tear into one another.

"You know, you should try that more often," she murmured, bending close to fill his cup. Bloody hell, it was all he could do not to lean forward and take a big ol' meaty taste of the luscious, cotton covered breast swaying just inches from his mouth, swallowing her down in one ravenous bite. He knew she'd taste like sin, and be just as deadly to his senses.

His lips curled in a snarl, his only defense against her. "Do what?"

She licked her bottom lip, watching his smoldering eyes follow the teasing movement, and the corner of her own beautiful mouth kicked up. "Smile. It almost makes you look half-human."

He tried not to watch her as she walked away, her gait as smoothly seductive and natural as the woman herself. For both his sanity and her safety, he needed to look away, but it was an impossible desire. Fuck, he couldn't keep his goddamn eyes off her. And he wasn't the only one aware of his preoccupation with the honey-blonde, gray-eyed mortal.

Across from him, Kieran made a humming noise of interest. "What's bothering you, Cousin?"

Lach growled, raising one dark auburn brow. "You have to ask?"

"I mean—the little American beauty, Lach. The one you canna drag your blasted eyes off."

He downed the fresh coffee like it was a much needed shot of tequila. "Keep out of it, Kieran. Trust me; I'm not in the mood."

His cousin's black brow mirrored his own. Kieran looked over at the woman, giving her a long, hot look that traveled all the way from her toes to the side part in her silky tresses. He whistled beneath his breath, the low sound filled with appreciative suggestion. "Now don't be gettin' all testy on me, Lach. She is a fine one, I'll give you that. Beautiful breasts. Nice ass. I like her coloring too." He looked back to his scowling cousin, smiling like the devil he was. "If you're not interested in her, man, I'd be happy to—"

"Don't even think about it."

Kieran slouched further into his chair, crossing his brawny arms across the wide width of his chest while he studied his cousin with curious fascination.

"You never minded sharing before."

"I do now," Lach growled, his tone betraying his unusual possessiveness.

"So it seems, Cousin. And does the mystery lady have a name?"

His entire body vibrated with tension. "Evan," he finally grunted, his reluctance to share even this much of her obvious in the biting enunciation of each syllable as it passed his lips. And he didn't like thinking of her by name, finding it necessary to keep that impersonal distance, needing the constant reminder that she was not *Magick*, but mortal, and thereby out of his reach. "Evan Hayes."

The woman in question reached up to pull down a mug from one of the top shelves, her sensuous figure stretching in a seductive arc that Kieran, as a lusty man, couldn't help but notice. He studied her closely, and all too easily came to an understanding of Lach's preoccupation with the little mortal. And was maybe even just that tad bit resentful that he hadn't seen her first. "So the lovely Evan's all your own, eh?"

The grooves went deeper, mouth compressed to an impossibly hard line. "No, she's not." But despite his words, his look clearly said otherwise.

"Hmm?"

Saephus, he couldn't take much more of this. Kieran was driving him outta his blasted mind, while little Evan Hayes made his goddamn gut ache with hunger, not to mention his friggin' cock. One look at her and he was loaded and ready to blow. It was fucking insanity what this mere mortal could do to him. But then, there wasn't a damn "mere" thing about her either.

"Hmm, what, damn it?"

"Has it not occurred to you that she might be the one?"

Just then Evan laughed with a man at the counter, giving him one of her warm, killer smiles, and Lach clenched his hands into fists, struggling to hold in his possessive need to blast the bastard into another dimension. He could read him as clear as day, his lust as evident as the smarmy smile spreading across his boyish face. Any second now and the weakling would get a load of magic right up his bloody ass.

With obvious distraction, he mumbled, "The one what?"

Kieran laughed beneath his breath. "For such a fucking genius, Cousin, you can be damn blind when you choose to be. The *one*, Lach. As in the answer to your wee problem with the Council."

Lach looked back at him, his shock easy to read for one who knew him as well as Kieran. "Did it escape your notice that she's a blasted mortal?"

"So? Who said your *bith-bhuan gra* had to be a Witch?"

"Excuse me?"

Kieran shrugged, ignoring the deadly tone of his cousin's voice. "I'm just saying they dinna say *Cailleach*. She doesn't have to be a Witch."

Lach's big, muscle-packed body shuddered with tension, and the lights of the café flickered above them.

"What the fuck does that mean?"

"It means, you stubborn ass, that your *bith-bhuan gra* could be just a woman."

Lach stared, his expression held tight, as if unwilling to let himself understand, and Kieran sighed with frustration. "A *mortal* woman, Cousin. Och, havenna you questioned why you keep coming back to this place day after day? And I canna say I've ever seen you stare at a woman, *Magick* or mortal, the way you've been eyeing that wee lass. I'm thinking the answer might be right before your eyes, and you're just being too fucking stubborn to see it."

A fine anticipation rippled beneath his skin, radiating power like the lethal grace of a panther as it paced its cage, awaiting fresh meat. Any second now and he was going to pounce.

"No." Just one word, rough with force, thick with fear. "No fucking way."

Evan looked toward them at the sudden outburst, and Kieran couldn't resist the temptation to wink at her, finding it too much fun to push Lach's buttons when it'd always been impossible to get a rise out of him before. Maybe this pretty little mortal was just what his too serious cousin needed. She blushed a pretty shade of pink at his obvious interest, but had enough spunk to return his smile instead of slinking away, and Kieran decided he liked her. Yeah, he was starting to get a real clear picture of why Lach had been skulking back to this place day after day, suffering the constant mortal contact.

"Get your fucking eyes off her or I canna be responsible for what I do to you, Kieran." The words were so guttural they were barely intelligible.

Kieran seemed to consider the threat—then gave another devilish grin. "You'd fight me for her, would you, even while saying she canna be your own?" His grin widened, black eyes bright with power. "Stop being a blind fool, Cousin. The lass is already yours."

Lach rose to his feet in a blur of movement—his chair tumbling back against the floor in a loud, scraping crash of wood against stone—and stared down at his friend and family, knowing that what he was about to say was nothing but the absolute truth.

"Lay a hand on her, Kieran, and I'll kill you. I'll fucking rip you limb from limb."

With that powerful threat, he tossed a ten note down on the table and stalked out through the door of the café, back into the bitter cold and the newly fallen snow. And despite the ache in his gut to take one last glance at her to hold him over till tomorrow, he never once looked back.

Chapter Three

Evan stood at the counter, nibbling her lower lip, two tickets to the Edinburgh Theater for the night's performance clutched in her hand. One of the café's regulars had something come up and so she'd offered the tickets to Evan if she wanted them.

She'd taken them eagerly. And though she loved the theater, Evan couldn't have cared less what the tickets were for, so long as they gave her the opening she'd been looking for.

She had to find a way to reach her *Magic Man*, because of all the men she'd ever known, he was the only who made her *burn*.

The only one who called to her heart and made her physically ache with hunger — like an empty, needy void within her that only he could fill. No matter that the gorgeous creature tormented her daily with his cold detachment and deliberate avoidance.

It wasn't that he didn't notice her. That was what drove her most crazy. So crazy that there were times it would've been pretty satisfying to tell the gorgeous jerk just to fuck off and kiss her little American ass, then go and find another sexy Scot to slake her lust. Maybe even the black-haired beauty still sitting at the table, studying her with those mesmerizing midnight eyes. He had a look about him that said he knew how to fuck a woman into oblivion, steeping her in pounding pleasure, but her goddamn body just wasn't biting at the bait.

It wanted Lachlan McKendrick. Case closed. No second choices, no matter how good they looked. It didn't care that he was the most infuriating man she'd ever known; it only cared that she get him between her legs, buried deep inside, and keep him there for as long as humanly possible.

A slow smile spread across her face at the thought.

Oh yeah, her body couldn't care less that he was a total shit. Three weeks of flirting with the tall Scottish stud and zilch. Not a goddamn thing. Nothing—except for that occasional look, the one she'd catch him giving her when he thought she wasn't paying him any attention. God, it was incredible. Dark and hungry and dangerous, like he'd do anything to have her naked and in his arms, his to do with as he pleased. Her cunt would go warm and creamy, drenching her panties, aching to be fucked, and all because the bastard had looked at her with those magical green eyes.

He tried to play it so cool, but it was those looks that always gave him away.

She saw those same looks in her sleep, when her sex-starved body would dream of him in vivid, heart-pounding detail and her throat would go dry from her cries of passion.

And to make it worse, she could see glimpses of the man he really was buried beneath the seething mask of discontent he wore like a shield, hiding from the world.

Hiding from her.

She wanted to know that man buried within the distant stranger. She *needed* to know him. For some bizarre reason, he felt like a part of her. Her body didn't care that they were strangers, didn't care their relationship consisted of little more than casual exchanges and carnal looks.

Hell, it wasn't all that concerned with the fact she had some serious doubts as to whether he was even human in the first place. She'd always been fascinated by the mystical, but she'd never known just how far into lust she could fall for someone who she was certain wasn't altogether human.

Not that she'd seen him sprout wings or perform magical acts of wonder, but there was an air of magic about him all the same. Something he wore like a second skin and it touched her every time he was near, like a whisper of sound, stroking her senses. It warned of formidable power and strength, but it didn't scare her. If anything, it drew her to him in a way she'd never been drawn to any man before. She'd called him Magic Man from the first day they'd met, and the name definitely fit. And after seeing how uncomfortable it made him, the teasing nickname had quickly become too much fun to resist.

But it didn't really matter *what* he was; she wanted him. He could've been the Jolly Green Giant for all her sex glands cared, and they still would've gone into cream melting overdrive every time she laid eyes on him.

He was hers.

Hers.

And now she was just letting him walk away again without doing a goddamn thing to move this thing forward. The beautiful black-haired one sat at the table, his glittering black eyes watching her like prey, anticipating her next move, curious to see what she'd do.

It *was* her move, and there really wasn't any question about what it was going to be.

You know what you want, honey, her hungry libido groaned. *Now go and get it!*

Damn straight, she thought, and it felt good to finally be taking some action.

By the time she hit the cobblestone sidewalk, he was already turning right at the corner. "Hey, wait!" she called out.

In her rush to reach him in time, she'd run out without her coat and the crushing cold ripped right through her, freezing her to the bone. But he'd stopped at the sound of her voice, standing at the corner, watching out of hooded eyes as she ran after him, and the look burning in those smoldering green depths almost made her forget the miserable Scottish winter raging around her.

When she reached him, her lungs were aching from the cold and she could barely feel her fingers. Of course, being a man, he didn't seem to notice. No, his green eyes had shot straight to the hard tips of her nipples, staring hungrily at the way they pressed against the thin gray cotton of her shirt. The greedy way he looked at her only made them pull tighter, until her breasts felt heavy and aching for the touch of his lips and tongue and teeth.

An uncontrollable moaning noise of physical hunger purred beneath her breath and his eyes ripped back up to hers at the erotic sound.

Then an answering grunt burst from his throat and he snarled, "What in the hell are you doing?"

Evan thrust the tickets into his hand, her cool fingers deliberately brushing against his hot skin. "I wanted to invite you to the theater tonight."

She watched as he looked down at the tickets, his light green eyes quickly scanning the scripted writing, beautiful mouth pressed into a grim line of determination. She knew he was going to say no and moved to beat him to the punch. "Come on, Magic Man." Her voice was a seductive purr, pouring over him, coating him in need, meant to drive him outta his goddamn mind. "I dare ya," she added with a teasing wink.

In a blur of movement, his hand shot out and he grabbed her, manacling her fragile wrist in an unbreakable grip that was only just shy of hurting her. She could feel the restraint he used, the leashed power thrumming beneath the surface of his hot skin against her own, and knew that despite his anger, he was still trying to be careful with her.

A delicious shiver spiked through her that had nothing to do with the weather and everything to do with the thrill of being at this man's physical mercy, just like in her dreams. She wanted to be laid out and penetrated, nailed to his bed beneath all those long, rippling muscles. Wanted to be shown in no uncertain terms just how badly he'd been aching for her. Wanted to be fucked till she passed out from the pleasure, reaching the kind of sexual heights she knew existed but had always had trouble attaining with her previous partners.

But her purring hormones told her she wouldn't have to try very hard with the prime specimen standing before her, no matter how much of a jerk he was.

Their attraction reminded her of two sculptures she'd once seen in a museum. On their own they would have been ideal and complete, freestanding, each a work of individuality without the other. And yet, when pressed together, they created something wonderfully different. A new form that uniquely strummed the senses while soothing the soul. It'd been a profoundly beautiful piece and she'd never forgotten it.

But it was that strange fitting of form that reminded her of how she felt about Lachlan McKendrick. Individually they were complete, but put them together and Evan knew that a thing of wonder would be created. And she didn't just mean cock to pussy, though she wanted that massive bulge behind the fly of his jeans so bad she could taste it.

No, it went beyond fucking to something deeper. It had to do with the way they would fit together in sleep and throughout the day. From the press of his body against hers to the way he'd hold her in his arms for the sheer joy of just touching her. The way her smaller hand would fit inside his much larger one. The way he'd hold her to his side as they shared his morning walks.

Christ, she didn't know how she knew these things, but she did. And it was driving her out of her goddamn mind. Why did she have to crave this union with a man who looked as if he were fighting a battle every time he laid eyes on her?

Hell, she didn't know what his problem was, and she was never going to find out if she didn't get through his armor and reach the man hidden beneath.

She watched as his lips pulled back over his teeth like those of a wolf when it growled. He was just as dangerous, just as menacing as he snarled, "If you know what's good for you, little girl, you won't ever fucking touch me again!"

Anger flared hot and deep within her chest. Who did he think he was—the conceited prick! For what was surely the hundredth time since setting eyes on the man, Evan wondered why she couldn't just let him go. Why him? What was his friggin' problem?

She jerked out of his grasp, but it was infuriating to know she was able to get free only because he let her. "I'll touch you if I damn well please." She stood straight and proud before him, her voice cool and steady, though inside she was seething with frustration, as much with herself as with him. "And in case you're blind, I'm not a fucking child."

"Coulda fooled me." He took a step closer, towering over her, too powerful to resist despite his arrogant attitude. "If I touched you," he sneered, his warm, deep voice hard and condescending, "I'd fucking break you."

With a forced indifference to outdo his own, she casually shrugged her slim shoulders. "Yeah?" she asked, rolling the word off her tongue in a husky drawl. "I'm sure I could probably go for the rough stuff as well as the next woman, but I'm afraid I only let men fuck me. I don't screw around with scared little boys."

He literally vibrated before her, a strange wave of heat crashing against her, as if she were blasted with a physical manifestation of his frustration, and she wondered not for the first time just what he really was. His big hands balled into fists at his sides, his voice little more than a rasp as he demanded, "What do you want from me, Evan?"

Other than his body pounding her into oblivion, she didn't have a clue. There should have been a thousand witty comebacks slipping off her tongue to put him in his place, but all she could think to say in her temper was, "I want you to go to hell."

She saw his beautiful mouth twist into a smile, but it lacked the warmth of the one she'd seen him give the black-haired stud in the café. No, this was a cold, mean, calculating smile; one she supposed was meant to drive her away as his eyes flicked over her once more. They were hot and hungry and full of lust, burning with an inner fire as he grunted, "I'm sorry to disappoint you, lass, but I'm already there." Then he turned and walked away, and she let him go.

Almost.

Suddenly the words were spilling from her lips before she'd even known she'd say them. "I dream of you."

He stiffened and stopped dead in his tracks, but he didn't turn around.

"Every night, I dream of you. And I wake up with the feel of you still throbbing inside of me. If that's not magic, Lachlan McKendrick, then I don't know what is."

She held her breath, waiting for him to turn back to her, only to see him walk away. Her teeth clenched and her hands fisted, angry resentment pouring through her till she felt sick on it.

How could he do this? How could he just walk away from this—this thing between them? What in the hell was he so afraid of?

Screw it, she thought. Christ, she'd already run after him once and spilled her soul, no freaking way was she going to chase after him again. Her body was just going to have to learn to goddamn do without; and her heart—well, she didn't know what its problem was. She wasn't in love with Lachlan McKendrick. Hah! How could she fall in love with a man she didn't even know?

But there was no denying the fact she wanted him in her bed.

Behind her, Kieran stood in front of the café, witnessing the battle of wills. It was clear he didn't need to be a *Magick* to see that the mortal wanted his cousin for her own. Hoping like hell he wasn't going to get his ass killed for this, he shoved his hands deep in his pockets and set off toward her as soon as Lach stalked away. He spoke quietly, but his deep voice was firm with conviction as he said, "He's yours, you know."

Evan spun around so quickly she almost fell on her backside. Kieran reached out to steady her, but she shrugged away, too pissed to be hospitable. "Great," she sneered, cutting him with her icy glare, "Another one. Do you guys travel in pairs, or what?"

He smiled at her fire, thinking of how much fun it was going to be watching this spirited little mortal keep Lach on his toes. "I'm his cousin, lass. Kieran McKendrick, but you can call me anything you like, seeing as we're going to be family and all."

Her slim frame vibrated with anger and cold and stunned disbelief. "Then how about Jackass, because I'm not finding this the least bit funny!"

"Good," he laughed, "because I'm not joking." Then he pulled a battered matchbook and pen out of his jeans' pocket and proceeded to write down an address in the McNeal Hills, one of the recently renovated, most high-priced areas of town. "He'll not be happy with me at first," he laughed, handing the address over to her. "But just remember his bark is worse than his bite."

"I wasn't aware he did happy in the first place. All I ever see him do is scowl," she grumbled, studying the scrawled address, wondering why this guy was sticking his nose into their business, even if he was Lach's cousin. Her chin lifted and she gave him a steady look, but his black eyes were unreadable. "Why are you doing this?"

The sudden flash of his smile was almost enough to warm the chill in her bones. "Because kin looks after kin," he drawled in his thick Scottish burr, "and there's more going on here than meets the eye." He nodded toward the matchbook in her hand. "Don't be too hard on him, darlin'. It's eating him up inside not to have you. And I canna help but think it must be hell on a man when he discovers he now belongs to a woman. If you want him, and I can see that you do, go after him," and then with a wink, he added, "I promise you, lass, he's all yours for the taking."

"Yeah?" she smirked, hating that she'd been so easily read. These McKendrick boys were a strange lot all right, and things were growing stranger by the moment. "And just what makes you think I want to take him anywhere?"

One black brow arched with obvious humor, making her grit her teeth, and he laughed, "Oh, so you don't want my cousin, then?"

Shit, she thought, it was too freaking cold to stand out in the snow and argue with the beautiful bastard. What was it with these McKendrick men anyway? Were they all like this? She tapped the matchbook with her nail, still studying him from beneath her lashes, trying to figure out his angle. "If I use this, then I owe you. What is it you want from me, Kieran McKendrick? You don't strike me as the sort who offers something for nothing."

He made a low guttural noise in the back of his throat, thinking that what he'd really like was something he couldn't have. The pretty little spitfire was Lach's now and he wouldn't touch her, but the temptation to do just that was like a fucking pain in his gut. Then the corner of his mouth kicked up in a wicked grin. "Got any sisters, lass?"

She gave a sudden throaty laugh, gray eyes sparkling at the hopeful note in his voice. "One, yes."

Kieran's dark eyes burned like black ice. "Och now, then I just might know a way you can repay me."

Chapter Four

The mortal was waiting for him on his goddamn doorstep.

He'd taken the long way home, trying to walk off some of his frustration, but it hadn't worked. And here she was, the woman of his blasted dreams, sitting like a pretty picture against the rough stone steps of his townhouse, fresh faced and smiling her siren smile. He thought briefly of turning around and heading away in the opposite direction, but the determined look on her beautiful face told him she'd only come after him.

"How in the hell did you know where to find me?"

Her smile widened, teasing and light, completely at ease. "Let's just say a little birdy told me."

Kieran.

"I'm going to fucking kill him."

She leaned back, elbows braced on the top step, magnificent breasts provocatively displayed between the open sides of her brown leather jacket. His tongue stroked the roof of his mouth in a restless gesture of hunger, eager to curl around the tips of her puffy nipples and suck till she screamed from the sharp stab of pleasure.

Her own tongue clucked, knee swinging side to side as if she had all the time in the world. "If I didn't know better, I might start to think you didn't want me here."

Lach ripped his eyes to hers, trying to quell her with the full force of his glare. "You should learn to trust your instincts."

She held his stare, her own gaze steady and strong despite the ache of desire pulsing through her. There was a heavy pull on her heart that she couldn't define—all she knew was that she was bound by it, drawn to this rugged man as if he were an extension of her soul, necessary for life.

Did he feel it?

Was this why he fought so hard to resist their attraction?

A glimmer of understanding began to take seed. This undeniable feeling of need was so overwhelming, it was like losing yourself, and she almost couldn't blame him for struggling so hard against it.

Almost.

"If you want me to go," she explained in a steady voice, "all you have to do is tell me to go. Tell me to leave you alone, Lach."

"Goddamn it, I can't do that!" he gritted through his clenched teeth. His eyes narrowed, drilling into her own. "And you know it, don't you?"

He didn't wait for an answer, but climbed the steep steps beside her and opened the huge oak door.

"Then why do you keep fighting so hard?" she asked after him, following him inside before he had the chance to slam the door in her face.

He ignored her, climbing the staircase on the far wall, his big boots heavy on the gleaming hardwood floors. The house was immaculate, the furnishings dark and antique, with a rugged edge of beauty that perfectly fit the man. He turned at the top to see her following after him, and lifted his brow at her impressive tenacity. "Maybe I don't like being chased by women?"

She couldn't help it; she smiled. "Well, I can't say I like the thought of you being chased by women either, but I'll take care of anyone who tries to get near what's mine."

His eyes flared. "Bloody hell! You just don't stop, do you?"

They'd entered the master bedroom, *his room*, and the sight of the immense king-sized bed set her already pounding heart to racing with dizzying anticipation. She watched him draw off his black leather jacket and boots, and then he moved toward her for the first time, probably trying to intimidate her right back out of his personal domain.

Too bad for him his little intimidation tactic wasn't going to work.

"No," she drawled, eating up his magnificent physique with her eyes. "I don't stop. Not when it's something important."

He took a step closer, blocking the light from the opposite wall of windows with his big, powerful body. "And you think two strangers fucking each other raw *is* important?"

Her lids lowered, shielding her expression. "It's more than fucking I want from you, Lachlan McKendrick. I think you know that."

"I don't think you know what you want!" he snarled.

The hell she didn't. "You're lying. We want the same damn thing!"

"Don't you think I'd touch you if I could, woman? I'd already have you nailed to the blasted wall with my cock shoved tight up your cunt, fucking your sweet little brains out, but I—*Fuck!* I have a problem and there's no easy way around it!"

Her eyes went wide, cheeks flushed with color. "Oh my God! You don't mean—"

Lach growled low in his throat. "Not that kind of problem, damn it!"

"Oh," she sighed, blinking in obvious relief. "*Thank God.*"

The animalistic growl continued to rumble in his throat, a warning of what was to come. "It isn't safe for you here, Evan. I'm not a normal man and you're playing at something that you know nothing about."

Her beautiful eyes went dark with challenge and she moved a step closer, unwilling to let him think she was afraid of him. "Then show me what you are, damn it! Stop running from me, Lach! I know you're not like me, but until you face up to this thing between us, we don't have a fucking chance of getting through it! The first time I laid eyes on you, I could see there was something different about you—some kind of power just waiting to be set free.

"I may not understand everything that's going on here, but I know what I feel, Lach. I know that I want you."

She reached out to touch his chest and he flinched at the contact as if she'd burned him with an invisible flame. "Whatever you are, Magic Man, I'm not afraid of you. Maybe I should be, but I'm not."

"And if I canna control it?" he thundered, towering over her, blasting her with his rage so that she could actually feel it against her skin like a warm gush of air blowing against her, surging around her body. Any second now and he'd be tumbling right over the edge. "I've been cursed, you little idiot! Every time I come, I shoot a load of magic outta my cock that turns the woman into a fucking animal! An animal, Evan! Are you getting the picture?"

A small smile played across her lips. "So you can make a woman go crazy on you, Lach? That's it? God, I could've told you that the second I set eyes on you. I may be human but I'm not a weakling, big guy. I can take it."

He looked as if he couldn't decide between laughing and shouting the house down. His eyes squeezed shut and he prayed to the gods for the strength to see this thing through. "I'm a cursed Warlock, Evan, and I'm turning women into *real* animals. As in furry with four legs, damn it!"

"Oh." Her face went blank, expression completely dumbstruck, but she wasn't running. Instead, she stood before him, silent and serious, obviously thinking the whole thing through, chewing on that goddamn luscious lip of hers. "Wow. That's—I mean—*Jesus*, I don't know what that is. Who would do such a thing to you?"

Lach didn't know what else to do but to answer her question, too tired of fighting to reason out why she was still here and not screaming down the street, trying to escape. With a ragged sigh, he leaned against the rough stone wall at his back. "I come from an ancient family of *Magicks*, Warlocks and Witches. My uncles are the family elders and they cursed me because they want me to find my *bith-bhuan gra*, or what mortals call their soul mate. If I come with a woman who isn't the true one, then the curse temporarily turns her into a bloody beast."

Her head tilted to the side as she thought about what he'd said. "Hmm. What kind of animal?"

"So far there's been a cat, monkey, goat, sheep, and a fucking Rottweiler, though I've been lucky not to have been inside any o' them at the time. But after the bloody dog, I don't think you'll find it too surprising that I havenna wanted to try again."

Her entire body shuddered as her vivid imagination conjured up image after bizarre image. "Jesus. I guess you can only be thankful no one turned into something hungry — with teeth."

He gave a short bark of laughter. "Oh, that last one had teeth all right. I've got the wound on my leg to prove it."

"Ouch. That must have sucked."

For a moment he just stared at her, unable to understand how she could believe him so easily. But she did. He could see it in her eyes, and he knew he'd underestimated her. Maybe she really did *know* him. "Among other things, yes," he drawled, "it did indeed suck."

She shifted from foot to foot in a restless gesture. "And it's because of this curse that you've stayed away from me?"

"Aye," he muttered, not looking the least bit happy about the admission.

Evan smiled. "Well then," she murmured, her look turning sly.

"Well then what, damn it?"

One shoulder lifted. "If the problem's just with you, you could always make *me* come."

He blinked down at her, his gaze so intense she felt it like a rough scrape of sensation against her skin. It was so hot she actually flushed at the raw carnality of it, a beautiful shade of pink painting her high cheekbones with color.

His hands fisted at his sides to keep from grabbing her to him, ripping her jeans off and ramming his cock so far up her cunt she could feel it threatening to break through the other side, as if he'd shove himself straight through her. *Saephus.* She was too fucking tempting to resist; this intoxicating combination of brazen and demure proving too much for him.

"No," he grunted, unable to say more without grabbing her and shoving his tongue straight down her throat.

Evan nibbled on her lower lip, the sight of her straight white teeth sinking into the tender flesh making him ache with hunger for a slow, deep taste. "Don't get all surly," she laughed with a wink. "I was only teasing."

He stood unmoving, deep gaze fixed on her, direct to the point of obsessive.

She shifted anxiously beneath such a blatantly ravenous stare, and her sly smile suddenly bordered on uneasy, conscience demanding she be completely honest. "Hell, it'd probably be a waste of time anyway. I've never really been that easy to—well, I mean I've *never* been *easy*. I just mean that I've never really had an earth shattering kind of, um—"

Jesus, she was rambling like a great blithering idiot here. And the intensely absorbed way he just kept staring at her wasn't helping her suddenly blabbering tongue. It was as though his light green eyes glowed with an inner flame, illuminated by the power within him. They burned on her, devoured her, as if he were anticipating her taste, bite by sumptuous bite; silent and hot and full of need. She took a deep breath, blowing it up through her bangs as she often did when she got flustered. "What I mean is that I've never been that easy to bring to an—um, to an orgasm."

Before the final consonant had fully passed her lips, his tall, muscle-packed body was pressing into her much smaller one, big hands gripping her shoulders, long fingers digging into the soft fabric of her jacket and the even softer flesh beneath it. The low, rough words growling from his throat were more beast than human. "I could make you come till it hurt, Evan! Make you cream till you begged me for mercy! *Begged me!* But I canna fucking touch you and not come all over you—and I won't risk you like that!"

The curse was dangerous enough to another *Magick*; who knew what it would do to a mortal? He'd rather die than cause her a moment's pain—and yet, even without the bloody curse on his cock, it would be difficult for a man of his size to fuck her and not hurt her.

But to never sink inside of her sweet little cunt would be his own personal hell.

In some insane way, this powerless little mortal had become the foundation of his reason for living, and he began to wonder if Kieran had been right. *Was she the one?* His power told him that she had to be, because she was the heart of his existence, his very soul. How could she not be the one? But how could he risk her if she was? What if she changed anyway?

He wanted to rage and fight against it as strongly as he wanted—no, *needed*—to cram himself inside of her, embedding himself so deep, penetrating her until he pierced her heart and claimed her forever! He wanted her bound to him in a way that would make it impossible for her to ever know another man again. Wanted her possessed, his and his alone, with a dominance of will that came as much from being a man in love as it did from being an arrogant Warlock.

She stared up at him with her ice gray eyes, her feelings open and honest on her face, everything exposed there for him to see. "*Lach?*"

It was as much a plea as it was a question.

Everything within him twisted with need, painful knots of hunger burning inside, and he clumsily shoved her away from him as his head spun and he fell to his knees. The ache was overcoming him, and he feared that he'd soon be too far gone to control the power's hunger for her. Not to mention that of his heart.

Evan stumbled back, catching herself on the foot of the monstrous bed. He looked up at her from beneath his brows, his glowing green eyes feral and dark. A strange movement shifted through his gleaming irises, as if a beast was prowling there, preparing to strike.

"Run." One word—dark, dangerous, hungry.

Run? Like hell. She'd come too far to chicken out now. Yeah, she was a little frightened in that *God, I really hope he isn't about to eat me* kind of way, but there was no fucking way she was backing out now. And even though she was just that little bit unnerved by his mind-blowing admission, she wasn't afraid of the man himself. He could be a Warlock or a Witch or whatever the hell he wanted, so long as he was hers.

She stood at the end of the bed and ran one hand through her hair, acting as if she had all the time in the world. Then she bit her lower lip in a slow, deliberate action and flashed him a challenging smile. "No, I don't think I will."

He growled in the back of his throat and a fine tremor moved through her, but she held her ground. Her fingers fluttered at her sides, and then she flicked the top buttons of her jeans.

One.

Two.

Three.

A dark, feral sound filled the room and then he was on her in an instant, his speed greater than that of any mortal man, and she was trapped before she ever reached the fourth. One second she was standing at the foot of the bed, and in the next she lay flat on her back, their clothes gone, her body bare and vulnerable while Lach's powerful thighs forced hers wide and his muscle-roped arms pinned her hands at the sides of her face.

"*Evan.*" It was a gasp, a grunt, a growl. "What in the fuck are you doing?"

She welcomed his weight, the delicious press of his heavy body against her own, and spread her legs wider, inviting him to take whatever he wanted from her. "Maybe I think you're worth a risk or two."

Lach screwed his eyes shut, hanging his head between his powerful shoulders, his hands clenched into huge fists around her own. "Damn it, Evan, you don't know what you're saying and I'm not going to be able to help you if this goes bad."

"But I do. Why don't you just try trusting me, Magic Man?"

He shuddered against her, the last of his control slipping through his fingers, and then his head was at her breast, his mouth hot and hungry against the lush mound, sucking her deep. She cried out at the shock of sensation while he worked the puffy nipple against the roof of his mouth, suckling at her as if he drew life from the fiercely erotic taste of her flesh. It was too good, the feel of her breast against his tongue, his teeth gently scraping around the firm mound, and he pulled away only to latch onto the other, drawing her in with deep, rhythmic pulls she could feel shooting all the way to the core of her pussy.

She went unbearably wet, dripping down the insides of her thighs, and he pressed the head of his massive cock against the swollen, pussy-pink lips of her cunt, nudging the tiny hole with a teasing stroke, giving it barely a taste of the delicious stretch that was soon to come.

Evan arched beneath him, a low, beastlike sound purring in the back of her throat, demanding to be filled and fucked. "Jesus, now, damn it! Don't hold back, Lach. I want it all. Every inch of it, right now!"

His muscles flexed, held tight with intent, and then he slammed into her, forcing the fist tight clench of her cunt to open and swallow him whole, rippling around him like a fucking little vise of pleasure. The feel of her was incredible, and he clenched his teeth against the need to spill his seed then and there, filling her up till she was coated with him, sticky and wet with his come.

"Are you on the pill?"

She shifted beneath him, her breath coming in rapid pants as she tried to assimilate the fact that she was stretched so wide and he was buried so deep. It hurt like hell because he was so massive, the granite hard shaft so long and thick, digging itself so far inside of her. But the dull pain was slowly beginning to recede and a throbbing ache for more was quickly beginning to take its place, demanding and insistent. "No," she moaned, needing him to move. "No pill."

"Fuck," he grumbled by her ear, his voice little more than a low rasp of sound, guttural and deep. "I'm sorry, lass."

His hips flexed, pressing even deeper, the huge head of his cock surging past her cervix, hitting a place that had never been penetrated before, and she moaned at the resulting jolt of pleasure/pain. "God, why are you sorry?"

He struggled to hold himself still within her, trying to allow her deliciously tight flesh the time to get used to him, but it wasn't easy. The need to hammer her rough and fast and deep was riding him hard, and any second now he was going to give in to it and fuck her raw.

It was almost unthinkable that he'd do it without protection, but he wanted to fuck Evan without anything between them. He wanted to fill her womb full of come and make a miracle with her so badly he could almost taste it. "I'm sorry because I don't fucking care if you're on birth control or not," he growled savagely. "And I'm not giving you a choice about it now."

She angled her hips, trying to take him deeper, and then flexed her inner muscles, smiling when he shuddered and growled above her. "Good, because I don't want one. All I want is for you to get on with it already!"

He gave a short bark of groaning laughter, loving her sass, knowing she'd always be strong enough to keep him in line and hold her own against him when his Warlock's arrogance got the better of him. He pressed a smiling kiss to her soft lips, teased gently inside the sweet heat of her mouth, and then he was gone.

His hips pulled back, his hunger for her taking over, and suddenly he had her hands pinned high above her head, holding her captive as he began a violent rhythm that had him shoving his thick cock in to the root, pounding through her gorgeous cunt till he thought the ecstasy of it would surely kill him. He was much too big for her, but she somehow took him, the carnal sounds spilling from her throat telling him how much she loved the feel of his cock hammering her so hard.

Evan arched beneath him, demanding everything he had to give. It was an addictive, raging bliss, because her *Magic Man* was fucking her brains out. His strong hips jack-hammered, shoving his cock into her cunt with brutal strength, filling the tight little hole to bursting. A thick, immense penetration. A delicious stretch beyond anything she could endure—and yet, she craved that feeling of being full of him, of that enormous cock breaking her open and fucking her, holding nothing back.

Christ, she couldn't get enough of it. Every time his body crammed itself in, forcing its way through her tight, drenched tissues, it was like a surge of power, as if he thrust her full of life. It glowed from her skin, a liquid illumination, and she could almost swear she felt it pumping from her pores with each meaty thrust.

"Oh God!" she cried, the hoarse words being ripped from her throat as a delicious pulse began to throb within her womb, spreading outward, soaking her in sensation. *"Oh Jesus, Lach, I'm going to come!"*

He cried out and his massive cock hit her high and deep, a thick ramming of flesh against flesh, the impossibly hard plowing into an unbearably soft, wet haven, and she screamed, her cunt gripping him so tightly it felt bruising. She came in a warm, sweet, clenching gush around him, and he couldn't bear it. His balls drew up hard and tight, painfully full, and he ground his jaw as the first wave ripped through him, scalding and hot and strong, pumping into her in a powerful surge as he slammed her with his cock again and again.

The bed rumbled beneath them, shaking upon its legs, banging against the wall as his magic poured from his body into her own. His heart stopped with fear and terrified sensation, all his formidable power focused on keeping her there with him, beneath him, and it was a profound rush of wondrous relief when she held tight to him, taking his come, claiming his future.

They shouted and ground against one another, the gut-wrenching sensations grinding down their nerve endings until they were drained and spent, clutching at one another in ecstasy, their skin soaked and smelling sweetly of sex.

A wide, satisfied smile broke across her face, while he grinned wickedly against the sensitive skin beneath her ear, teasing it with slow strokes of his tongue. The curse had been broken, the hungers of the flesh momentarily fed, and a love more powerful than all the magic in the world discovered at last.

Lachlan McKendrick had found his *bith-bhuan gra.*

Chapter Five

"Um—Lach?" Evan whispered just a moment later, her voice sounding strangely tentative after the mind-shattering intimacy they'd just shared.

"Yeah?" he groaned, his own voice harsh, ragged and out of breath.

"Who are they?"

"Huh?"

"Who are they?"

"Who's who, sweetheart?"

"These—um, five old guys with long beards who are staring at us. Not that I'm a prude or anything, babe, but I *am* a one man kinda woman."

His entire body went tense above her, every muscle going hard in shock and disbelief. He turned his head to the side and cracked one eye, unable to believe what he was seeing. His uncles were there all right, grinning like loons, obviously as pleased as punch with themselves. "I don't fucking believe this," he growled, reluctantly pulling his still hard cock from her sweet, clinging depths. His body curled around her, shielding Evan's naked flesh from the five sets of curious eyes looking on. "Get out," he snarled. "Get the fuck out!"

Seamus tsked from his post at the foot of the bed. "Och now, Lach. Don't be gettin' all testy on us, lad. It's no something we've ne'er seen before." Evan peeked a wide-eyed look at him over Lach's broad shoulder, and the old man's grin widened, his bushy gray brows wagging mischievously. "Mind you, I canna say I've ever seen one as fine as this."

"Seamus, take your goddamn eyes off my woman or I canna be held responsible for what I do to you." Lach struggled for the edge of the sheet, doing his best to keep Evan covered beneath him. "And that goes for the rest of you too. Get the fuck out o' our house!"

They laughed and clapped each other on the back, saying "*Our* house! Did you hear the boy say *our* house?" followed by "Told you he'd come around, I did. Just had to find the right lass to make him settle, he did," and then a "He'll be thanking us for this when he's no longer worrying about giving us a wee peek at paradise, now won't he?" which was rejoined by several enthusiastic shouts of "Aye, he will." Lach clenched his teeth together so tightly his jaw began to ache.

Knowing the only way he was going to get rid of the nosy old biddies was to blast them from the room—so he could get back to more important things that involved lips and tongues and sweet, slippery juices—Lach carefully pulled the sheet up over his back, then rolled to his side, keeping the soft fabric tucked tightly around Evan.

She smiled at him, her face flushed from coming, looking so beautiful it made his heart ache, as well as his cock. Saephus, he loved her, and he was going to spend the rest of his life proving it to her in sinful, explicit detail.

He leaned down and placed a warm, wet kiss against her soft lips, smiling because he couldn't seem to help himself. Shit, he'd probably spend the rest of his life grinning like a jackass, and rightfully so. The gods knew he didn't deserve her, but that sure as hell didn't mean he wasn't keeping her.

"I have to get rid of the pests, but I'm nowhere near done with you yet," he warned.

She laughed huskily, running her fingers through the silky locks of his hair. "I should hope not, because *I'm* not done with *you* either."

He kissed her again, unable to resist the sweet temptation, the fever in his blood that only she could ignite beginning to boil all over again. Evan moaned and the kiss deepened, consuming them, pulling them under like a violent force of nature until they heard the gleeful snickering coming from the other side of the room. His uncles were huddled together by the large stone hearth, rejoicing over their success, heads bent in private council, planning Saephus only knew what. Lach pulled reluctantly back from the intoxicating taste of her mouth, relishing the fact that hers was the only flavor that would ever pass his lips again.

"I better get them out o' our house before they zap the whole friggin' family here."

Her lids lowered over questioning eyes. "*Our house?*"

Lach tipped up her chin with the edge of his fist. "Aye, *our* house. Tell me you havenna been thinking I'd ever let you get away from me, Evan. I'd kill any man who ever dared to touch you. *You're mine.*"

Her arched brow lifted in an arrogant imitation of his own. "And are you mine?"

He lifted her hand and pressed it to his heart, letting her feel the rapid beat that came just from having her near. "In this life and the next, sweet. I'd never touch another woman, be she mortal or *Magick*, for anything in all the dimensions, ever again. And I canna think of anyone more special to belong to than you."

Her eyes went hazy with love and lust at the heartfelt admission, marveling at what kind of wondrous fate ever decreed that she be the lucky woman to own the heart of so wonderful a man. It mattered not to her whether he was mortal or *Magick*, only that he loved her and always would.

Knowing the truth of her words was already shining in her eyes, she replaced the press of her hand against his heart with a soft, sweet kiss from her lips. "I love you, Lachlan McKendrick. Always and forever, I'm yours."

His arms wrapped around her like steel bands, securing her to him, his body trembling as the words rushed up at him. "Ah, Evan, I was wondering when you were going to get around to telling me that. I hate to admit it, but it's been giving me some bad minutes wondering if I was ever going to hear those words from you."

She smiled against his chest. "And?"

His arms squeezed tighter, and then his hands moved into her hair on either side of her head, tilting her face up to his. "*And* I love you too, lass. Och, I always have. Why do you think I've been so bloody scared to be near ya? I havenna trusted myself not to toss you over my shoulder and steal you away, so I could have my wicked way with you."

She licked her lips, trying to focus through the haze of desire. "Speaking of having your wicked way, do you think we could get some privacy before I have my own with you?"

Lach's eyes flared, shocked at the realization that he'd momentarily forgotten about his meddling, obnoxious uncles. He looked over to find them all watching with wide-eyed fascination, the lot of them hanging onto their every word, smiling like a twittering group of old women. Saephus save him. He made sure Evan was still covered and then rose to his full height, standing tall and proud and unashamedly naked beside the bed.

Evan blushed for him, but then she figured when you looked as gorgeous as Lach did, you really didn't care if people saw you clothed or naked as a jaybird. Of course, the only woman who was ever going to see him in all his magnificent glory ever again was herself. And it was a view she planned on enjoying and taking complete advantage of for all eternity.

Lach stalked across the room like an angry wolf preparing to fight for his territory, but the five old men just kept on smiling, as if they didn't notice the danger burning in his light green eyes. No, they were too busy taking stock of his cock.

"Och now," his Uncle Reggie remarked with enthusiasm, "I told ya the boy took after our side o' the family."

Lach rolled his eyes at the outrageous comment, the corner of his mouth lifting when he heard Evan trying to stifle her infectious giggles behind him. They might drive him out of his bloody mind, but at least his family was sure to provide them with their fair share of humor in the years to come.

"Aye," his Uncle Iain readily agreed. "They all do. Why do you think they've been so blasted hard to settle down? It takes a lusty wench to be able to satisfy a pri—"

"Enough!" Lach roared, trying not to laugh; his heart smiling for him at Evan's choked gasp behind him, her laughter muffled by the covers she'd apparently pulled over her head.

She peeked over the edge of the sheet just in time to see Lach throw his arms up into the air, muscles bulging, rippling down his back in an impressive display of strength, and then there was an immense crash of thunder overhead that she could've sworn sounded like the heavens roaring. Across the room from her, his uncles' eyes bulged as wide as her own.

"He's come to it, then," the one named Seamus called out over the resonating cracks of thunder. "I told you old fools he'd tapped into his power in its entirety. Thank Saephus he finally claimed the pretty little lass there or it could've been the end of us all."

"*Out!*" Lach roared. His hair whipped around his head as if he were caught in the center of a violent windstorm. "Leave now, or like I warned you before, I canna be responsible for what I do."

He lowered his arms, pushing them forward, and the blast of wind rushed against his uncles, sending peals of proud laughter up to the sky.

"Fine, fine," Seamus called out as they gathered their long, ancient cloaks around their still powerful bodies. "But we'll expect to see you for dinner on Sunday. We can perform the Binding Ceremony then."

A streak of lightning cut through the room, blinding Evan as she watched the strange tableau from the safety of the bed, and then his uncles were gone in a crackling flash of light, and she was alone once more with her *Magic Man*.

He turned back to her, his eyes burning hot, and she could feel the hunger coming from his body, crashing against her in warm, erotic waves of promised pleasure. "Are they gone?"

"Aye," he growled, climbing onto the end of the bed and slowly crawling over her, his huge cock hard and ready to fuck, the wide, blunt tip already streaming with juices. He gripped the sheet in one strong fist and ripped it away, sending it to the floor as his eyes fastened on the juncture of her closed thighs.

She watched as he licked his lips and had to bite back a groan. "And are we going to dinner on Sunday then?"

"Aye," he drawled again, his nostrils flaring as he smelled her delicious scent on the air, strong and sweet and feminine. "But I'll be eating you now, if you havenna any objections."

Evan took a deep breath as anticipation spiked through her, sharp and sweet, setting her body to a fine tremble. She parted her thighs, lifting her knees out high at her sides, loving the stark, ravenous look that fell over his face as he looked down at her open, glistening cunt. She was primed and ready, hungry for his massive cock, dripping with cream and aching to be fucked.

With a teasing smile, she reached down and circled the tiny hole with the tip of her finger, slowly dipping inside, and then pulled it out of her clinging depths, rolling her hips with the erotic movement. Her finger glistened, shiny with sweet tasting cream, and she lifted it to his lips for a decadent taste.

Lach opened his mouth and drew the juice soaked digit between his lips, sucking it, his senses clenching and cock crying at the honey sweet taste and smell of her cunt.

Evan pulled the slender finger free and he grunted, "*More*," holding her thighs spread wide as he shoved his face straight into her, his tongue digging deep with the first plunge. One thumb found the ripe, almost bursting bud of her clit and pressed hard, roughly stroking it, while the other found the sweet little hole of her ass and pierced deep, shocking a hoarse cry from her throat.

He laughed into her; a dark, dangerous sound of arrogant satisfaction, looking forward with savage anticipation to the eternity of fucking they had before them. He'd happily spend it right here, pressed up tight against her pussy while she flooded his face with cream, filling his belly with love and lust and the sweet, faithful taste of their love.

"Come," he ordered into her. "Come for me, Evan, right down my fucking throat like you have in my dreams!"

The harsh, guttural command sent her tumbling straight over the edge, her body writhing, cunt pressed shamelessly to his face, pumping against his wicked mouth and tongue. And then in a blur of movement she was pressed hard to the wall, pinned by his hard-muscled body, her knees held wide over his elbows and his cock buried up to her eyeballs while he fucked her into an endless, screaming climax that pulsed through her blood like a rush of flame, scorching her with its pounding intensity.

He must have used magic to get them there so quickly, her nailed to the wall and penetrated within the blink of an eye, and she smiled at the lucky fortune of having this beautiful *Magic Man* who'd stolen her heart all for her own. Yeah, she was a lucky girl indeed; but then, she planned on making him feel pretty lucky too.

"I love you," she moaned breathlessly, his beautiful cock still fucking the hell out of her, hammering her with love. "*I love you.*"

His lips found hers, his mouth claiming possession of the sweet, moist recess as thoroughly as his cock claimed her cunt for his and no other. "I love you too," he grunted, his lungs laboring for air. "So much it bloody hurts. Promise you'll never leave me, Evan. We're bound forever, lass, and I'd die if I lost you."

She kissed him sweetly. "I'll never leave you, Lach. I'll always be yours."

"*Always,*" he growled, taking the kiss deeper.

And then her *Magic Man* sent her crashing over the edge of ecstasy all over again.

About the author:

Rhyannon Byrd is the wife of a Brit, mother of two amazing children, and maid to a precocious beagle named Misha. A longtime fan of romance, she finally felt at home when she read her first Romantica novel. Her love of this spicy, ever-changing genre has become an unquenchable passion — the hotter they are, the better she enjoys them!

Writing for Ellora's Cave is a dream come true for Rhyannon. Now her days (and let's face it, most nights) are spent giving life to the stories and characters running wild in her head. Whether she's writing contemporaries, paranormals…or even futuristics, there's always sure to be a strong Alpha hero featured as well as a fascinating woman to capture his heart, keeping all that wicked wildness for her own!

Rhyannon loves to hear from readers.

Also by Rhyannon Byrd:

Against the Wall
Waiting For It
Magick Men II: A Bit of Magick

Once Upon A Midnight Blue

By Shiloh Walker

Once Upon a Time....there lived a soldier who had served the king faithfully for many years, but when the war was over...

Chapter One

Before The War

Aric dropped down on the soft bed beside his current woman and snuggled into her soft curves. She sighed and pressed her lush plump ass against him and he groaned, smacking her hip as he said, "I must wake early, Deria. Go to sleep."

The youngest Master at Arms Edouine had ever seen, his duties asked much of him. But he did them faithfully, and gladly. His King was a good and just man, and he honored him. He would never sleep if the King asked it of him, if his body allowed it. He felt Deria pout and she muttered, "Always you wake early. You place the duty to your King above all else."

Aric hardened his voice and dug his fingers into her hip. "I am a solider, Deria. And a citizen of Edouine, as are you. The words you say are evil. We must all place our duty to our King above all else." But he was a hypocrite. There was one thing he would have gladly put above his service to the King, and that was his yearning for the King's daughter. The Princesse Amery.

Amery...his cock hardened and he rolled Deria onto her back—spread her thighs, pierced her cleft and shoved inside. She wiggled and giggled in surprise, then gasped in startlement as he started to push into her hungrily, unaware he was seeing another face in the darkness. Aric groaned raggedly and came quickly, uncaring that Deria had just started to lift her hips to his. He pulled his wet cock from her pussy, and held Amery's face in his mind. As Deria gaped at him in the dim light, he said gruffly, "Be mindful of how you speak, Deria."

* * * * *

Aric knew he watched her like a lovesick pup. He had only once before spoken to her and she had been a child at the time, only thirteen. He had just been the Master at Arm's apprentice, and she had been kind and gentle, stumbling upon him after he had taken a beating for daring to question the Master's honor. She had been exploring in a part of the castle where she should not have been and had used her gift of healing where she should not have used it—on the ragged gashes in his back.

They had not spoken before or since, but the love he felt in his young man's heart had started then and only grew. He hid it well, though. It would not do for the man so recently appointed Master at Arms—and under such scandalous terms—to be known to openly adore the Princesse. When his Master, the man who had beaten him a decade earlier, had died of a heart storm, his duties had fallen to his apprentice, Aric. Aric had not been expected to take the position for decades yet but such a mess had surrounded the former Master's death, the King had not wanted any more upheaval.

Especially since it had been his sister, the Princesse Elva screaming bloody murder that had aroused the guards who had found Master Swenson dead. She had rolled over in the darkness to take his member in her mouth…if she had bothered to light the candles first, she could have saved herself quite a fright.

That had been just the King's sister. She had been rushed away to a distant family holding in shame. Lowering herself to cross the line between Castes— fucking one of her brother's servants—even one esteemed as the Master at Arms. If even a word was breathed how much Aric craved the Princesse Amery, he would pay dearly. He watched as the lady crossed the yard to the stables. She would hardly recognize him now. Perhaps she'd not even remember him.

She had just returned from college, learning to control her healing skills, learning the skills she would need when she became Queen. If no worthy mate was found, she would not marry. She could take a consort to father a child in order to have an heir, but she must find a worthy mate in order to marry.

The Caste system. Aric's lip curled in disgust. He understood the system well. Understood and hated it.

His place in the system was unknown, to be true. Those outside the Caste had no mark. A birthing mark separated the worthy from the unworthy, all people born in the Caste system had a mark, or so they were taught. Aric had a half mark, low on his belly, shaped like half of a star—a pale, pale blue. He had been found, the lone survivor in a nasty carriage accident when he was a young child. It was assumed he was the child of a noble lord and for a while the church had cared for him, expecting family to come for him, but none ever had.

So he was fostered out. He couldn't be thrown to the streets because he was Caste. But no one knew exactly where, thus no one wanted to take responsibility. When he was nine, a weapons master discovered he had a knack for fighting and took him in, and slowly made sure that he caught the eye of those who mattered. By the time he was fifteen, he was the apprentice of the Master at Arms, and Aric knew the weapons master was responsible.

Moments later, he briefly lifted his eyes from the men training to watch the Princesse Amery and her retinue, accompanied by the guards he had personally selected, set out for her daily ride. She paused briefly to nod and smile at him and he bowed low, hiding his surprise behind a blank, respectful mask.

She remembers me.

The battered boy had grown into a man who was so sensual, so handsome it made her belly tighten. Amery resisted the urge to turn her head and look back as she followed the guard in front of her into the woods. She had thought of him, far more often than she should during the years she had been away. She had thought of him far more than she should, period.

He no longer had to keep his hair cropped close. Befitting his new rank, he had let it grow, and it had grown down nearly to his waist, a black straight banner that had blown around in the light spring breeze as he watched his men train. The black jerkin had been sleeveless and worn over his naked chest. If he practiced as his predecessor, then by the time she returned, he would shuck the jerkin and be half nude, covered in sweat as he grappled and fought and threw the men down.

They would fight him harder. They would feel they had to, because he was young, and he was handsome, and his Caste was unknown. Some of the men he trained were knighted, some were nobles. Master Swenson had been the second son of an earl, a very high Caste. Nobody truly knew of Aric. They would give him trouble, she thought, brooding. *Why does that bother me?*

She wanted to see it, though, even if it bothered her that they would fight him and try to hurt his magnificent body. He had such *kind* eyes. And kindness wasn't something Edouine bred. Ruthlessness, brutality, rich and fertile lands, all these things Edouine bred well. But not kindness. She sneered as she thought of her step-father, the King. King Alhdeade had not a kind bone in his body. If there was truly fairness in the world, he would have been born outside the Caste, and never would have been mated to her mother after Amery's father had died.

And if her mother had the sense the Goddess had blessed a goat with, the Queen Halah would have seen behind the mask Amery had known was there. But so very few saw past it. So very few.

Even Aric was fooled.

Chapter Two

The War

Aric studied his King's haggard face and knew the older man was going into battle whether Aric argued or not. Alhdeade was, and would forever be, a warrior. "We are losing, Majesty," Aric argued. "Take the Queen and the Princesse and go to your family in the North. We will lose Edouine City — but not Edouine itself. The Army will not fall. Why risk yourself?"

"The Queen and Princesse are already in the North. I received word this morning," Alhdeade assured Aric as he held out his arms for his page to finish strapping his armor. "But when you ride out, I ride with you, Aric. You have served me well and faithfully these past five years. But do not think that gives you the right to question me."

"I would not see my King at harm," Aric said, falling to one knee, lowering his eyes.

Alhdeade smiled and said, "I know, my friend. But these are my countrymen that are being slaughtered by Akkerites. I will not stand by and watch."

Aric saw the tiny black creature dart across the road while they camped. He frowned absently, but ignored it. He knew what it was. A smoke elf. The tiny little fey creatures were drawn to war and havoc, but weren't dangerous to the living. In fact, if treated well, they could be quite handy. He had read tales of the little fey rendering entire armies blind and deaf and allowing their foes to reign in victory. They chose the party who was ill-favored, with the good heart, so Aric wasn't worried they were here for mischief.

But he wasn't prepared for some of the superstitious louts he had under his command. He had been propped on his pallet, smoking *shai*-tobacco in his pipe, just outside the Royal tent when the shout went up. He heard the loud, pitiful cry and felt the sick fear inside his belly. He heard the King's sleepy voice, "What ever is the awful racket?"

"Remain in your bed, Majesty, I shall see to it," he said. And he hoped he was not too late to keep some bad omen from befalling them.

The King, however, did not remain abed.

Aric found three of his men tossing the tiny pitiful little winged creature around like a child's toy. It couldn't fly away. Two of the four wings were broke. He caught it mid air and snarled at them, "Fools! Have you no sense?"

The King was moving toward him and tossed the creature a dismissing glance. "A fey? Kill it, Aric, put it out of its misery."

"Kill it?" he repeated, dumbly. "You don't kill the fey." Aric stared at his King in horror while he stroked the tiny, shivering back. The creature was no taller than his arm was long, his skin blacker than the night, with pointed ears, a fine downy cap of curls and soft, pale crystalline eyes.

"You'll have to, unless you want it killing you while you sleep, Aric," King Alhdeade said quietly, shrugging his shoulders. His grizzled face saw the horror on Aric's face and hardened. "You cannot allow that pitiful creature to jeopardize our camp, Master at Arms."

"If our men hadn't harmed the fey, we wouldn't be in danger, Majesty," Aric said quietly, lowering his eyes respectfully. He cradled the tiny thing in his arms, studying the battered face. "What am I to do with you, little fey?" he asked quietly. "I know not how to kill an innocent creature. I was raised with honor."

Alhdeade's face hardened and his eyes narrowed but the tiny creature's mouth opened and the voice that came from it was like the music from an angel's harp. "No harm, I bring, I meant to bring no harm. But to kill a fey will bring death to all," it sang. The tiny little man stared up at Aric as though mesmerized. "Such kind eyes you have, mortal. Not of Edouine, completely, are you? The Akkerites will slaughter you, people of Edouine. Came to help, the fey did. And look at how you treat their emissary."

A soft low keening sound left the little creature's throat. Many of the eyes of the soldiers dropped away with guilt, for they had laughed in amusement at the poor thing's shrill pleas. Others had felt pity but had said nothing. Even Alhdeade's eyes filled with guilt and self-disgust, and he had thought he had pushed beyond such emotions.

"It's a fucking monster," a lower Caste noble rasped. He had been the one who had grabbed the fey and started to torment it, seeking to raise himself in the eyes of those around him. Some of the voices around him hummed in approval, wishing to rid themselves of the guilt that flooded them as the creature spoke. "It is not even human—no blood bond, no Caste, no god. It is nothing."

Aric glared at the man who spoke. Quietly, he asked, "Majesty, am I still Master at Arms?"

"Have I ever said otherwise?"

Aric inclined his head. "You, take your belongings and remove yourself," he said to the one who had spoken. "And thank the Goddess I do not kill you. If we lose this war, you had best pray to her that I die, because if I live, know I hold you responsible. This creature, this noble fey was sent to help us. And you cost us that help."

The elf laughed. A tiny, pain-filled sound, but a laugh all the same. "Aye. He cost. But you brought it back, Master at Arms. Such kind, kind eyes."

"If I had been truly Master, I would have found you when first I saw you and brought you to my fire. I would have foreseen possible trouble and protected the noble fey," he said formally before beckoning for the Army's Healer. He was vaguely surprised when the King sent his own instead of the general population healer.

"Those with a good heart always believe those around them have good hearts as well," the fey said. His nearly translucent eyes darkened to navy with his pain as the healer ran his weathered hands over his broken body.

"A frail body you have, little fey," Cyrus said with a sigh. "I know little of fey anatomy. Will I harm you with my lack of knowledge or can I heal you safely?"

"Not necessary—if you will just grant me some strength, send myself to home, I can. My own healers, I need. Poor set wings mean I will never fly," the little fey said it quietly, a mournful tone. He lifted his sad eyes to Aric and forced a smile. He cupped his tiny hands blew into them, and blew and blew. Then he opened them and revealed a tiny little gem.

An elf mark. A great gift. Aric shook his head. "I cannot accept that," he said shaking his head rapidly.

"You can and must," the smoke elf said, solemnly, though a hint of a smile lingered on his face. "I will argue until you do, and the longer I must argue, the longer I must suffer. Must I suffer, Master at Arms?"

Aric sighed and reached out, folding his hands over the tiny golden gem. It glittered like a golden diamond and the moment he touched it, it moved itself into his flesh. "There, it will stay, until the day you truly need it," the noble fey said. "And when you need it, you simply call, and I shall come and whatever you ask of me, it shall be granted."

The day of the great battle came. Aric stood at his King's side, weary, angry, and disheartened. Alhdeade was not the grand man Aric had thought. Over the past eight months he had learned that. But he had sworn to fight this war to the end. And he would see it done. He feared for his men, he feared for his country.

And for Amery.

"You sound so weary, my lad," Alhdeade said quietly.

"I am weary," he said bluntly. His eyes itched and burned from staring into the night. The final front was mounting. The Akkerites had been surprised by how fiercely the Edouinites had battled for the country, for the King who didn't deserve their loyalty. "I am ready to go home."

"Soon. Tell me, boy. What would you ask of me, for your faithful service? I would have not come so far without you. Indeed, I would not be alive without you," Alhdeade said.

Amery. He kept his lips compressed and shook his head. "I merely wish the war over. I want to go home."

A roar broke open down the line and a strong ripple of magic filled the air, followed by the stink of blood and brimstone and evil. The Akkerites had done something evil — a demon walked the night.

Aric knew they would need help this night, and called silently to the fey. A burning pain ripped through Aric's hand and he bellowed as the golden elf mark tore from it and the tiny little creature — no longer broken and battered — appeared before him.

"Oh, tis you, the Master at Arms...so sad you seem. The war is heavy within you. But still the love for the lady is in your heart," the little smoke elf sang in his oddly dulcet tones. "What would you have us do?"

"Let us not suffer defeat," Aric said numbly, holding his pained arm to his chest.

"Us? What's the creature doing here? What lady?" Alhdeade said, hardly aware anything had happened on the line.

"He has a yearning for the lady himself," the elf said, his tiny face wrinkling with disgust. Aric couldn't comprehend. The lady? Amery was his child — what? The elf disregarded the King. Nobody disregarded the King. "My brethren come. Not the smoke — we are too small, though we are many. Look for the giants and the winged ones. And beware the King. He bears you no love."

The little smoke elf was suddenly gone.

And outside, the screams started.

Chapter Three

Betrayal—After the War

Aric hadn't expected to be made an earl. Or even a knight. But he would have liked to have gone home.

Instead he was left to die on the side of the road. Alhdeade paused to look down at him and clucked his tongue. "You served me well enough, but I've no need of you any more," the King said as Aric lay sweating through the fever that had followed the infection from the spear he had taken in his side.

The battle had raged swift and bloody for less than one night. Centaurs and giants had swept in and destroyed the demons and the Edouinites had swiftly conquered the frightened Akkerites. Aric had found himself battling four cornered knights who he had seen rush the King in desperation, and thus the wound. For the first few days, he had received quite the Royal treatment.

Then it had, inexplicably, stopped.

The infection passed after three days of raging fever but he was starving and hungry and weak and angry. He would return home, all right. And he would find a way to make Alhdeade pay. He'd not have won the war without Aric.

The little hut ahead of him wavered but he kept on. He stumbled onto the porch as it grew late, and he banged weakly on the door. It opened to reveal a woman uglier than sin and he pleaded weakly, hating how low he had fallen, "Old woman, I beg of you, some water, please. Some food."

"The war done with you, eh? I've not much, but if you will stay and work a while after you heal, then well, all right..."

The first month passed slowly and he was hardly able to do little more than water her garden. But then the nasty old hag insisted he care for it as well and Aric followed her orders. What choice did he have? He was too fucking weak to wander the roads still, and if he tried, well, some nights the fever from the wound still came back, and the old woman was handy with potions, even if she did like to leer at him.

As his strength returned, Aric grew to hate the old woman, but he had also become indebted to her, and enslaved. The bloody woman was a fucking witch, and the nights she had been treating his fever, she had been taking the blood she had spilled from his body. She had his blood, she had his hair—she had not his name, and thank the Goddess for that. But she had power over him and he couldn't just walk out, even though he no longer suffered from the recurring fever.

"When may I leave?" he demanded for the third night in a row after he had been there nearly six months. "The garden is all prepared for winter. You've food enough to last you *ten* winters after all the hunting I have done."

"But no wood," the old woman mourned. "No wood at all. How will I cook the food? How will I keep myself warm?"

Aric bit back the need to tell her she most likely could shoot fire from her shriveled old ass if she saw fit and merely conceded, "I shall chop the wood. Then may I take my leave?" By the Goddess, he wanted away from here — away from this desolate land, away from the memories of his humiliation, away from all of it. He wanted, one last time, to see Amery. And he wanted vengeance on the King for his betrayal. Then he would take his leave of Edouine — if he lived long enough.

And he wanted a woman. He retreated to his pallet behind the blanket he had strung, his cock hard and aching as it had been for months. He waited, though, until he heard the old woman's snores before he freed his cock from his trousers and closed one hand over the rigid engorged flesh. The ruddy head was swallowed by his hand as he started to pump, lids drooping to half mast, as he imagined it was Amery's silky little pussy, or better yet, her mouth. He had to bite his lip to muffle the groan as his hand picked up in tempo — until his seed splashed onto his belly, burning hot and wet.

Oh how the mighty had fallen, Aric thought wryly as he cleaned himself up and burned the little rag. Damned if he'd allow the witch to have any more of his bodily fluids. There had been a time when he had the most expensive courtesans warming his bed, and even some higher Caste wives had sought him for a quick fuck, all discreetly, of course.

And now, he was resorting to pleasuring himself merely for a little relief.

Soon. He made the promise to himself. He would get away from the bloody witch. He would have his vengeance on the King, and he'd find a woman on the way to sink his aching dick into. He pulled his old pipe from his shirt and filled it with a tiny bit of what remained of his fragrant *shai*-tobacco — puffing a bit before he tapped it out and went to sleep.

The wood was chopped.

"One last favor, I beg of you, soldier, before you go. I've dropped my light — it is such a special light — into that dry well, and I am far too old to fetch it. You've been too ill until now to get it, but before you go — "

Aric stared at her, resigned. "Your word," he said finally. He wouldn't have dared to ask, if he wasn't so desperate to flee this place. But he could not possibly stand another week here. And winter was coming quickly. If he didn't leave soon, he may not be able to leave for months. "I want your word, and your bond and your blood seal that after I am out of that well I may have my leave of you, without tricks or strings or promises."

Her faded eyes flashed with anger before she smiled ever so sweetly. "Of course," she cooed, sounding like a sweet old grandmother.

Aric wasn't fooled but he went to the well and sure enough, he saw the blue light. "I do not understand why it has not yet burned out," he said, frowning a bit.

"It is a special light, not true flame. It never truly burns out," the old woman said. "But it works only for me. Now, hurry and fetch it, soldier. Don't you wish to go home?"

Aric flashed the witch a tiny smile and swung his leg over the lip of the well, using the rope and weak toe holds to work his way down. The ground below was boggy, and a bit damp, but the well was basically dry. His hand hovered over the blue light, which gave a cool sort of heat, but did not burn him so he scooped it up. "How am I to carry it?" he shouted up.

A tiny golden box was flung down to him and he put the light into it—the blue light dancing within the golden walls, spinning around with a mind its own. The longer he watched it, the more it looked like a flame, and the warmer it began to feel. "Come, come, we haven't all day, now have we?" the witch cried out.

He grabbed the rope and started to climb, but it was far more difficult to go up than down—the toe holds worn, the walls slippery and treacherous. When he neared the top, she said, "Give me my blue light."

Narrowing his eyes at her, he said, "Not until I am on the ground."

"Give it to me," she snarled, reaching for him.

Aric wrapped one wrist in the rope to secure himself and easily batted her hands away, laughing. "You healed me too well, old woman. You'll not be getting it from me until I choose to give it to you. And I'll give it to you when I am on firm ground again," he told her, his pale green eyes glinting with amusement, his thick black braid falling back behind him.

She hissed and spit and raged, slashing at his face with her ragged nails. All that, Aric didn't mind. But then her hands started to glow, with an eerie green light. So he did the sensible thing and released the rope, falling to the soft, soggy ground below. And when his head cleared, the rope was retreating up the wall and he was well and truly stuck in the fucking well.

"Well, shit," he snapped, banging his head against the wall. His gut burned and twisted with anger. At the witch, for not being honest. At the King, for lacking honor. At himself, for being a fool and trusting others. And now he was going to die down in this bloody well—cold and wet.

Reaching into his pocket, he opened the little golden box. It was almost hot to the touch and the blue light was more flame now. Wondering, he prepared the last of his *shai*-tobacco and checked to see if the little flame was indeed fire. It was, and produced a terrible smoke.

But, *ahhh*, the warm, fragrant smoke filled his mouth and lungs, and Aric leaned his head back against the stone wall, and closed his eyes and drew the smoke in again, unaware more smoke was pooling and thickening all around him, then condensing and forming into a solid being. A very *solid* being.

Aric's eyes opened as two thick, muscular thighs were forming and his pale green gaze widened in shock, his numb hand falling from his lap. Within moments, he was staring at a much larger version of what looked to be a smoke elf, but it was huge, and had only one set of wings.

The man cracked his head one way then the other, his crystalline blue eyes the same color as the flame that had enslaved it. He flexed his massive wings as far as he could within the tiny well then stared up, a smug smile on his face. Then he looked down at Aric.

His voice was deep and throbbing, like water rushing over stones deep underground. "I know of you, Master at Arms, Aric of Edouine. You saved the noble fey, my kin, Serian. You are known among us, and you could have used the elf mark for any wish—riches, power, anything, even the Princesse you yearn for—yet you used it to save your people."

Aric was rather pleased he was able to speak calmly, when his thoughts were rushing around his head, babbling like something quite insane. "Know me?"

The huge creature—he must have towered over Aric by more than a head—smiled as he hunkered down and touched the tiny starburst mark on Aric's hand—left by the elf mark coming out of his skin. "Aye, we know of you. Serian told you, kindness does not come oft out of Edouine. You make a habit of saving the fey, it would seem," he said, eyeing the tiny gold box, the pipe. "The witch has been holding me inside that flame for ages. It's my transport form but she enslaved me in it, and until another freed me, I could not come outside. I could still converse with my kin, but another mortal had to free me. And not just any mortal, but the one who was to be my true Master."

Looking at him speculatively, the creature stated, "And that would appear to be you."

Aric shook his head slowly and said, "I am no man's master, not any longer. I am barely more than a servant, especially the last few months."

The man smiled, his long tightly curled hair slithering around his massive shoulders as he cocked his head and said, "You freed me. Only my intended Master could have done so. She thought *she* was my Master, and only her hand could do it. But when she tried to pull me from the flame, it did not work. In her anger, she flung the flame down here, and I have been trapped for nearly a millennia. Hundreds of men she has sent to bring me. Sadly, all who have tried have failed. The spell she put on the flame drove many men to insanity or instant death—I owe her much pain for that. She used me as a weapon."

Then the elf smiled, his wings slowly fanning the air, as if he could not tolerate to stand still after being so long confined. "Ah, but now—now I am free, no longer trapped. How did you come to be here? I know of what went on with you while you had the elf mark from my kin, Serian, but what after?"

"I've been a bit trapped here myself," Aric said quietly, pushing to his feet. Yes, a good head taller, and Aric was not a small man. The Master at Arms stood easily over six feet, but this massive creature dwarfed even him. "I made the mistake of knocking on her door for water after taking an injury."

"An injury? Why were you not treated by the King's own physician and healers? Are you not the hero of Edouine?"

Aric snarled, his pale eyes going hard and cold. "One might think thus," he hissed. "The King turned me out like a fucking mongrel dog, to starve and die."

"Ahhh. And you are angry," the massive elf said quietly. "I blame you not. I've my own anger. But I pay the witch back well simply by escaping, and taking you with me. I am at your command, Aric, Master at Arms, friend of the noble fey."

Aric's clenching hands stilled and he stared at the elf. "My...my command?"

"Aye. You released me. I'm no smoke elf. I am demi-elf and my talents, and desires, lie truly in finding a human companion to serve." A slow smile slashed his face, white and glowing. "I can think of none better. I grant wishes, well and true, and I offer good advice, whether you ask of it me or not. And whether you want me or not, I am at your side. I spoke only truth. Her spell was cast that only my Master could free me. I was meant to bond to one mortal, for all time, to serve, to befriend, to advise. And that, Aric, friend of the noble fey, is you."

Aric studied the handsome, towering man in front of him—clad only in the long fall of inky, black hair, a loin cloth, and his massive wings—and shook his head. "I've no way of caring for myself, even I were to get out of this well—"

He had barely spoken the words and they were outside the well. His head was spinning and he stared at the demi-elf who was leaning against the well, smiling sunnily. "At your command, Master at Arms," he repeated.

They heard the wailing scream of anger from inside the house and Aric turned to see the witch come running. He felt the impotent anger he had suffered the past months breaking loose and with a feral smile, he said, "Then I command you, see this woman receives the punishment she deserves, not just for her crimes against me, but for the crimes I am sure she has done to others."

The elf and the witch were gone. Aric was only alone for a few seconds—his hair was still blowing from the breeze the demi-elf's departure had stirred up—and then the elf returned, alone. "Do you know the witch has been out hunting the small children? Trying to find those with power, and when she finds them, she drains their life blood?" the demi-elf asked conversationally. "That is how she has survived this past nine hundred years, while she strove to break through and master me and use my magic to prolong her life. She has survived all these centuries by stealing the lives of children."

Aric blanched.

The elf smiled. "I just wanted to make sure you didn't suffer guilt when we go through the town and you see the charred remains of her corpse in the town proper."

"You mean it. You truly mean you are at my command," Aric said quietly, staring at the being in front of him.

The elf lifted one massive shoulder. "I had been out searching for my mortal — the one worthy of my service — when I was unlucky enough to be captured. How did I know you had not yet been born? But, yes, truly I mean it."

"For how long?"

The elf smiled a secretive smile, as he said, "A very long while. There are things coming in your future that you know nothing of, young Master at Arms. You will need an advisor you both like and trust."

Aric lifted a black brow and said, "Whoever said I trusted or liked you?"

The elf threw back his head and laughed heartily. "You do not, not yet. That will come, in time."

Aric felt an unbidden smile curving his mouth. "I believe I need a name to be calling you, then don't I?"

The elf smiled and said, "Blue."

He eyed the creature, black as the blackest ink, from head to toe, the only relief his eyes, his rather red mouth, the flashing white of his teeth when he smiled, the pinkish moons of his nail beds, and the rather startling length of his white nails. His body was long, muscled, and pitch black, like a statue carved from ebony, dipped in black gold, glistening, and perfect. But not blue.

"Blue you are most definitely not," Aric said slowly.

Blue laughed again. "Come, we must be going. It is home you wish to go, is it not?"

Chapter Four

Shame

Aric stopped at the inn, smiling coolly at the innkeeper, his fine clothes marking him as high Caste. Blue was in the golden box, where he preferred to travel when in the city. The fey weren't feared, and they weren't generally treated the way poor Serian had been, but Blue didn't particularly like people, especially city people.

So when around people in the city, he would fold his massive form into his magic one—the tiny blue light—and Aric carried him. The fine clothes had come from Blue, as had the gold and more of the good *shai*-tobacco. He had offered a better pipe, but the old one had been a gift from Aric's first weapons master and he wouldn't give it up.

"Know you yet how to seek your revenge?"

Aric's shoulders tensed and he replied silently, *"I truly wish you would not talk to me this way. I will eventually reply out loud and people will think I am daft."*

"Then they will know what I already know," Blue responded easily. *"I have heard odd whispers, how the Queen has died and the King wishes to replace her with a new Queen. There are whispers of scandal. Shall I investigate?"*

"No. I have a job for you. I want the King's daughter. Here. Tonight." Aric's anger had grown greatly over the past weeks. It had taken them little time to come here—Aric suspected while he had slept Blue had been using fey

magic to shorten the trip. He cared not, but his rage had grown, his hunger had grown.

He felt Blue's surprise. *"Are you certain? If you are caught, it could mean your death. To bed a higher Caste, if her blood relatives wish your death, then, so be it."*

"If I am caught, I expect you will save me."

Blue laughed and said, *"Of course I will. But is this the way?"*

"I have hungered for the King's daughter for years. Why not take her, especially if by doing so, I can take my vengeance on him? And," he mocked coldly, *"did you not point out to me that I could have used your kin's elf mark to take the Princesse I yearned for? If I had done so then, I would not have suffered so."*

Blue studied the sleeping girl. She appeared to have been crying. He had an uneasy feeling in his belly, and wondered if he should have questioned Aric further on this, but Aric had a kind heart. He was angry now, but his anger would lessen, and he would not do anything too traumatic to the girl.

From the look of it, she was already traumatized. Anything his Master did would be an improvement, Blue decided, eying the bruise on her cheek, the bruises on her wrists.

He lifted her, closed his eyes, summoned the fey magic and they were in the finest suite at the inn, which he, of course, had magicked against any eavesdropping. He laid the girl gently on the bed, brushing her hair away from her face, caressing an ivory cheek with the back of his hand before he tossed Aric an unreadable glance. "She looks sad, Master. She's been—"

Aric smiled, small and mean. "I'm not going to rape her, Blue. Just wake her. I want my rooms cleaned. My boots shined. And I want her to remember."

He flopped onto the window seat and pretended to read. He should have been rejoicing in this—he should have been able to kick back and laugh and jeer at her as she slaved about his room. So why did he feel so ill inside? Why did he feel so very guilty?

As her eyes drifted open at Blue's command, he had to leave. He couldn't watch her act the menial, even if it was all to shame her father. Surely, she would be telling her nurse and the King would hear. And it would continue. The King would come to question the odd happenings.

Aric would shame the Princesse, but bring her no true harm. At least, she wouldn't be left to suffer and die on a roadside.

But still, as she stared around the room, her lovely face awash with confusion, Aric shot to his feet and left, even as his cock lengthened and hardened and demanded he go to her and take her—take his vengeance inside her sweet, young body.

Amery woke early the next morning. She remembered the past night, the dream that seemed so real. She stared hatefully at her captor, her 'nurse' as her step-father called Sajera and slowly repeated the dream, how she, a Princesse Royal had cleaned and shined boots for a high Caste lord who had long black hair.

She was unaware that Blue was listening and laughing silently as the nurse repeated the story to the King later that day. The King followed the advisor's words and sewed seeds into the pockets of the Princesse's sleeping gown later that night, "In case it happens again, Majesty. With the wedding close, we want no trouble," one of the advisors said solemnly.

She lay on her bed, dismal, depressed, missing her mother who had died in the North during the war. Missing her carefree youth and her innocence. She had so little time left.

Closing her eyes, she slept. She was so tired. It had to have been a dream, but she felt, truly, as though she had cleaned and worked all night. And it was odd. There was a blister on one hand.

"Did you watch her today?" Aric said, walking into the sleeping chamber from the bathing chamber. He was going to fuck Amery. He had bathed and planned and plotted.

"Aye, Master. She slept. She told her nurse and her nurse told her father. They think to sew seeds in her pocket to leave a trail," Blue said, laughing from where he lay on the floor drawing little rainbows in the air with one ivory nail. One wing was folded up, to keep from being lain on, the other was partially curved over his body while he played with his magic.

"Do you know that since I was sixteen, I wanted one woman, and only one?" Aric said, sitting beside the elf, his body going hard, his eyes fogged by hunger. "She was still very young and a Princesse Royal, something I could never have. But I wanted her."

"Then you shall have her. But do not do it to be cruel to her father," Blue said in warning. "I do not think that is fair to her."

Aric slanted Blue a look. "And was he fair to me? Bring her to me, Blue."

Blue rose with a slow, liquid movement, the long lines of his ebony body gleaming in the dim light of the room, his wings moving slowly, the faint tracery on them catching the eye even when not looking directly at them. "And where am I to be, Master?"

Aric lifted a brow. "Unless it truly bothers you, I prefer you to be here. Watch if you choose, ignore if you do not. But I'd prefer you to be handy in case something goes wrong," he replied.

Blue smiled, his eyes heating as he flexed his wings. He still preferred to wear only the loin cloth and under it his massive cock swelled. "Oh," he purred. "I like to watch."

Amery was half awake when the creature came, so she knew it had truly happened. She started to struggle when he lifted her, but he turned mesmerizing blue eyes on her and breathed into her face. "Sleep, little Princesse. I take you to a man who desires you like no other," he crooned.

She struggled even more. Though still virgin, the past few months had taught her to fear a man's desire. Her step-father and his cruel hands as he 'persuaded' her…she screamed, but the action had no sound and then they were just gone.

When she opened her eyes she was in a rather opulent room, the walls covered with gold silk, a huge four-postered bed with more gold silk, blankets and fat pillows. A man, vaguely familiar, reclined on it watching her.

"I do not like the gown, Blue. And the seeds are annoying me."

Amery shrieked as her gown disappeared. It was replaced by something soft and gossamer, not sheer, but close. She heard the man behind her laughing, his black as coal hands soothing her shoulders gently, trying to calm her. "There are seeds all over the streets now, Master, in every shop and inn. I wonder how that could have happened," the man behind her said.

"Come," the man on the bed said, sitting up and staring at her.

Amery couldn't believe it when her feet moved. A soft, foreign voice caressed her mind. *"He desires you, loves you. I feel your need for him, but I also feel your fear…I cannot allow you to fight him, Princesse. It would cause him such pain and guilt when he looks back, and he deserves his vengeance."*

She didn't stop moving until she was on the bed straddling him, staring at him with confused eyes. The other man, the dark creature, was still at her back. And the man who looked vaguely familiar was suddenly more so. Aric, the Master at Arms, whom her step-father had claimed died during the war.

"You will service me tonight, Princesse—not I you," he said, moving her from his lap so that she knelt in front of him.

She didn't see the disapproving glare that flashed from the elf to the man, as she stared uncomprehending at the cock he was revealing. She knew what a man's penis looked like, and she knew what the basics were, but what did he expect her to do? *"Lick his flesh, Princesse like that,"* said the voice inside her mind as an unseen hand guided her head.

She licked her lips nervously, staring up the length of his body at him, the muscled plane of his belly, the carved perfection of his chest as firelight danced over him. The muscles in arms flexed and shifted as he reached out with one hand and cupped the back of her head, wrapping a skein of silky red hair around his fist, nudging her mouth closer to his cock as he narrowed his eyes at her, those pale slivers of green flashing hungrily, dangerously.

Desperately. *Desperately? Why should he look so desperate?* Amery thought in a half panic as she tried to tug away from him.

"Stop clouding her mind, Blue," Aric snapped in command. "This isn't a lover's interlude." Amery's eyes widened as he pushed his shaft inside her mouth. He was thick, hard, and salty. To her shock, she felt wetness pool between her thighs.

"Perhaps I could at least offer the lady pleasure?" Blue asked mockingly.

Aric groaned raggedly but since he didn't refuse, Blue moved to the Princesse and she moaned around the cock that was surging in her mouth. She had pleasured herself before, and often, but her slim fingers couldn't quite offer what a man's could. The creature, no—Blue pulled her gown up and started to circle his finger around her clit, while the other hand came from behind to rim her open slit, which was wet.

"She enjoys pleasing you, Master," Blue said, his voice hoarse, his face buried in her red curls. "She is wet and aroused. Does she not deserve pleasure and not shame?"

"What about what I deserve?" Aric rasped but he pulled away—need, shame, anger, all roiling inside him.

Amery couldn't think as Blue started to thrust his fingers inside her wet cleft, virgin tight, slick with cream. Her eyes widened when Aric knelt in front of her, his face harsh with desire, hunger, and anger. A tearing sound ripped the air as he tore the lovely gown from her and lowered his head. But then he stilled as he caught sight of her averted face, and his breath caught in his throat.

"Blue, she is bruised."

"I realize that, Master. But she is close to coming, and it would be cruel to deny her that," he said, plunging his fingers deep, circling his thumb around her clit.

Amery felt tears of shame fill her eyes, trying to bury herself against Blue's massive chest when Aric cradled her bruised face in his hands and kissed the mark on her cheek before he slowly moved down to her breasts, where he took one swollen nipple in his mouth, then the other, before moving slowly down on her body, groaning in anguish.

"Stop, Blue. I will bring her to climax, I swear. I have to taste her," Aric said, ordering his man to stop—taking the Princesse and spreading her on the bed. Blue moved with them, sprawling beside them, reaching out and cupping one round breast as Amery sobbed with need, her small hands clutching the black elf to her, but he caught her hands and held them down gently while Aric moved between her thighs.

"He seeks to give more pleasure…to taste your sweet body," Blue murmured, staring down the long slim white lines of her. Her breasts were round and soft and pretty, firm to touch. He took a nipple in his mouth, aware that Aric watched. When his Master didn't tell him to stop, he proceeded to suckle and nip while Aric used his fingers to spread her folds open.

Amery quivered when she felt the cool brush of air. Then the hot wet caress of his tongue. She cried out, felt him drive it inside her weeping passage before returning to suckle on the hard bud that brought such pleasure while he drove two fingers inside her pussy. A tightening inside her groin grew and grew until it broke—like a dam breaking—a river seemed to flow from inside her. Aric groaned greedily, and the dark elf echoed the hungry noise as he slid one hand down to stroke the slick wetness that coated the outer lips of her sex and thighs before bringing his fingers to his mouth, pulling from her nipple to lick the cream away as he murmured, "What a sweet little prize you are, Princesse."

She pulled away from both of them, curled onto her side and started to cry, deep wracking sobs. Aric curled his body around her, feeling misery and shame surging inside him. "Why are you shaming me this way, Aric? What did *I* ever do to you?" she demanded through the tears.

"My lady Princesse—you? Nothing, but your father, the King…" Aric sighed, brushing her hair away. "He took everything, and in my anger I lost my head. I struck out in rage, and since I have always wanted you, I decided to take you. I must beg your forgiveness. Blue can erase this memory and return you to your rooms. I will not trouble—"

"Do not call that bastard my father," she snarled in a low hateful voice.

Aric's hand stilled as he stopped brushing her tangled hair back. "I know that he has angered me greatly, but what has he done to you?"

She laughed, a low bitter sound. "Have you not been back in Edouine City long, Aric, Master at Arms? Have you not heard? In three weeks time I am to wed him."

"He is your father," Aric rasped, sitting up slowly, staring down at her face.

"Not by blood. And I am the Queen's blood heir. In order for him to stay on the throne, he must wed me, or he loses the kingdom," she said. "He married my mother after my father died when I was two. I am the rightful ruler of this land, but by our laws, I cannot claim it until I am twenty eight, which isn't for another six months. Six bloody months. It might as well be six years."

He reached up and touched the bruise on her cheek. He touched her wrists. "Did he do this?"

"He did. I refused him, heartily and vigorously, but then he started to put people to death. First a prisoner or two, then a servant who spilled something in the kitchen, or a page who didn't deliver a message timely." Her eyes filled with tears. "By our law he has the throne for six more months while I try to find a worthy mate. And he has sworn that unless I decree it to be him, Edouine will run with a river of red."

Blue's breath left him in a rush, while Aric turned her face first one way, then the other. The fading bruise on her face and those ringing her wrists were visible marks but he had had no idea how deeply the internal scars went. "Has he forced you to his bed?"

She shook her head. "No. He will take a Royal virgin to his bed this time," she mocked, deepening her voice and affecting her step-father's brogue. "His advisors suggested he go ahead and bed me, while I sat there, to secure the throne. But he was certain I'd stick to the agreement. After all, he has six more months in which to kill my people. And unless I can find a worthy mate...and who is high enough Caste that the people and the church will accept him? They will find fault with all but a King or a Prince and none dare to come here, for Alhdeade has been known to kill them, or allowed them to be killed in recent years.

No foreigners dare to enter our borders any longer, particularly none of high enough Caste that I could hope to find a mate. And I am not allowed to leave Edouine to find him on my own."

Blue was smiling as he sat at the foot of the bed. Aric caught sight of that smile and frowned. "*There is nothing amusing here, Blue.*"

Blue's smile only widened.

And a rather malicious smile was curving Amery's mouth. "*The Princesse has thought of something that amuses her greatly, Master,*" Blue relayed as he sat up. Folding his massive body as small as he could, he draped his wings over the back of the bed as he watched the Princesse straighten up and stare down at Aric.

"I have no choice but to wed the King Alhdeade. Unless a Prince Royal from another country sneaks into my country and makes an offer for me, and how likely is that? She rolled onto her side and slid Aric a glance" she stroked one finger down the center of her body. "You brought me here to shame me, thinking that I am the King's beloved daughter, when in truth he wants me to be his Royal whore. I will shudder and try not to scream every time he touches me. And I can think of no greater vengeance — for myself, nor for you — than to disallow him the Royal virgin he wants on his wedding night."

Aric tore his eyes from her slim finger as she slid it through the red curls between her thighs to stare into her bluer than blue eyes. "I am not worthy of such a fine gift."

She smiled slowly. "You are. And I deserve better than to spend my life under a rutting old man. Don't I deserve at least one night? Especially since I dreamed of you for years and years. I wept when they reported you had died, Aric, Master at Arms. I had so many dreams of you," she purred as she swept her finger back and forth over her clit.

Blue moved off the bed—allowing them space—retreating to the wall. He continued to watch, but he forced himself to divide his attentions as he sent out a summons to his many kin. There was a great deal of work to be done and so little time…

Aric slid his eyes back down to where she was touching herself, the pearl of her clit plump and swollen, slick and wet with her cream. "Is this not shaming you?"

"Not if I am wishing you to do it," she responded. "Not if you are not doing it simply to shame me. Do it out of desire, even love. The noble fey says you have love in your heart for me—is that true?"

Aric raged silently at his companion but he turned to face the Princesse, his pale green gaze glittering in the dim light, his black hair falling in its loose braid over his shoulder as he shifted onto his knees to stare into her eyes. "It is true, fool that I am."

She reached up and painted his lips with her cream, causing him to groan and lick it away, catching her hand and licking the cream from there as well. "Virgin, how can you be virgin?" he wondered, drawing her slim, sexy body to his, cuddling his throbbing cock against her belly.

"I feel a great deal in my heart for you as well. I do not know if it is love, Aric. It fluttered every time I saw you, and I wept when I thought you were dead. And the thought of never seeing you again made me sad. I am still angry with you—I am suffering with that. I do not know what the love for a man feels like, but I do care for you, and I want to feel you inside me, at least once."

Aric used his weight to push her to the bed, knowing from a glance they had too little night left. "I will give you what you wish, if you will allow me a boon. One more night in exchange. Allow Blue to bring you back for one more night," he asked. "We can't linger tonight. We've wasted too much time with my being petty, and I hungered so much. Dawn will come and your nurse will find you gone. I dare not endanger Blue."

She shifted beneath them, spreading her thighs. "Take me tonight, *now,* and I will come back as often as you wish it, as often as I can, even after I am forced into a marriage I do not want. If your Blue can spirit me out of my locked bedroom now, he can surely do it then," she whispered.

Aric smiled half-heartedly. "You will not want me for long, my Princesse." He would see the King dead before he allowed such a marriage to take place. And seeing to it would probably cost him his life, but ah, well. He lowered his head and caught one peaked nipple in his mouth, glancing out of the corner of his eye.

Blue was watching, that strange little half smile on his face. With a shift of his body, Aric moved so that the elf could see more clearly as he slid one hand down Amery's body to cup her mound, plunging his finger deep inside. She was so wet, so silky, so ready for him.

He wasted little time—he had hungered for her, and time was short. Mounting her, he whispered in her ear, "This will hurt you, Amery." Her name. He whispered it again, just to say it.

She cuddled against him, wrapping her arms around his neck she whispered back, "I would rather the pain come from your body taking mine than any other." She bit her lip as he took his cock in one hand and started to possess her, slowly, pushing his thick shaft into her wet, tight sheath. When he came to her virgin's shield, he stopped, shuddering. He lowered his brow to hers, wanting to weep with the pleasure of it. "I've wanted to be just here," he whispered, pressing down just a little on her clit, "for so many years."

Then he pulled out, lacing one hand with hers as he crushed his mouth to hers, biting her lip roughly. When she jerked back, he pushed through the fragile membrane, taking her innocence, swallowing her short cry, and soothing her tense body with his own—stroking her back, worshipping her lovely breasts with his mouth, sipping from her red nipples—while he stroked and teased her clit. "You like being touched here. You've touched yourself here before, have you not?" he asked, teasing her, coaxing her through the pain.

"Mmmm. And I loved the feel of your mouth on me." Her eyes, bright with tears, slid to Blue. Her face heated, but Aric watched as her eyes shone hot with excitement. "Your companion...watches us."

"Blue, the Princesse—"

Blue moved closer, still smiling that lazy, sardonic smile as he knelt beside the bed. "Your Princesse is a hot young lover, Master." Blue watched as Aric moved until he was kneeling on his haunches between Amery's spread thighs. The flickering firelight danced over the muscled perfection of his battle-scarred body, the sweat gleaming on his arms, shoulders and chest as he slid his big hands around her hips and started to pump his cock in and out of her tight, narrow cleft.

Aric's head fell back, his long black hair falling almost to the bed as he groaned, the planes of his face hollowing as he grimaced in sweet agony at the feel of her tightening around him. The muscles in his belly bunched and shifted as he pulled out then worked his cock back inside her snug little pussy, the half-star of his Caste mark seeming to gleam faintly in the room.

Blue lowered his head to Amery's breasts, taking a rosy nipple in his mouth, he suckled deep before whispering gruffly, "Tis almost a pity she is such an innocent. There are pleasures two men can give such a sensual woman."

Aric pushed his cock deep inside her satiny pussy, groaning at the picture spread out before him. Amery's dark-blue eyes closed, and her deep-red hair spilled out over the gold of the silken sheets mingling with the dense black of Blue's hair as his companion drew the Princesse's nipple into his mouth. Her long, slim, pale torso contorted and contracted with her shuddering breaths and he felt his balls draw taut as he watched himself push inside her tight passage. The slick bud of her clit, he caught between his fingers and rolled, plucked, stroked until she was crying and screaming his name as she started to tighten around his cock in climax.

He waited until she started to come, then he did— with a rough, low groan that rumbled out his chest, crying out her name, his fingers digging into her hips, and dragging her up and down against his cock, letting her squeezing contractions milk his come from him—his head thrown back, the veins standing out from his muscled neck while he shuddered with the pleasure of it.

Blue was breathing raggedly as he sat up, staring at them while Aric lowered himself to the bed, curling up behind Amery. She lifted her lids and stared up at Blue. And asked in a low, smoky voice, "What kind of pleasures?"

Aric started to laugh. "The kind of pleasures a virgin should not take her first night," he responded.

Blue smiled, a tighter smile this time, moving away from the cool hand that brushed over his thigh. He *would* have moved away, but she pressed down and he obeyed the silent command. "What of tomorrow night?" she asked.

Blue's eyes widened with surprise, a look Aric rarely saw on his face. Cuddling against her firm ass, Aric considered it. "Perhaps…"

She rolled onto her side and slid Aric a glance. "Your companion is still unsatisfied, Aric." Then she lowered her head, pushing his loin cloth aside, and the rolled cloth that covered him, taking his length in her mouth. Aric felt a flare of jealousy and Blue started to pull her away.

"No. Her choices, all," Aric commanded. He shifted onto his knees behind the Princesse eyeing her exposed naked ass, the way her position opened her sex, the pucker of her anus. "The other pleasure is here," he murmured, licking his finger and pressing it against her anus. "A woman can take a man in her bottom and feel pleasure like I cannot tell you."

Her body shuddered. He pushed the fat head of his cock against her wet cleft as she slid her mouth up and down half of Blue's massive cock, while the elf groaned in ragged pleasure. "Is that the sort of pleasure you wish, Princesse?" Aric asked as he thrust deep inside her cleft from behind. He cried out as she took him deep, clenching down around him and squirming against him.

He stroked his hands over the curves of her ass, watched as her head bobbed up and down. "I cannot hear her thoughts, Blue. What does she wish?"

"She wishes very much…to try it, Master," he groaned, pushing his hips up, wrapping one hand in the lady's red curls, rocking against the wet caress of her mouth. "I had…not expected such a…reward."

She smiled around the cock in her mouth, arching back against the one inside her vagina. Aric slid one hand around and stroked her clit. The hungry thrusts of male bodies were such an erotic thing she felt her pussy clench in hot anticipation. And her mind, the angry pride of an insulted Princesse Royal took satisfaction in the insult she was dealing her step-father. She stroked one hand down the thick, warm length of the elf's black cock—blacker than pitch—wrapped her fingers as far as she could around the base and started to pump instinctively as he pushed harder against her mouth. She felt a hungry moan in the back of her throat as Aric pounded into her harder, pinching her clit, but she couldn't voice it around the flesh that was pushing past her lips—sliding farther down her throat, and she took him as far as she could without gagging, trying to pull away, but his hands locked into her hair, and he cried, "My lady, please," as he started to pump. A salty flood filled her throat as he came—rocking deep, as deeply as she could take him—while she shuddered, her own climax breaking, and lasting forever, trying to find it's way out of her in a scream, but she couldn't scream because Blue's large cock was in her mouth.

Aric pounded into her, shoving her hips lower, staring at the sight of Blue forcing her to hold still and take the thick black cock down her lily white throat as he came—he saw the alien excitement in her face, felt the clenching of her body as she came—and he spewed his semen deep inside, bellowing her name, then rasping it out weakly when he could breathe again.

"I am sorry, Master, but I must take the lady, and we must go *now*," Blue was saying moments later.

Aric barely had time to kiss her, aware that she still had the taste of another man's climax on her mouth, and then she was gone.

Moments later, the rushing wind signified Blue's return and the elf was staring at him with blank eyes. "Am I to beg forgiveness?" the elf asked.

Aric could hardly comprehend this noble, exotic creature. Amery had given Blue something of her own free will. Blue served Aric of his own free will, for Aric still didn't understand this *bond* Blue spoke of.

Aric didn't feel he owned this very dominant creature, didn't feel he had the right. Blue was a noble, dignified man, one of the noble fey, an ancient, glorious race that made the mortals of the world seem petty and mongrel, yet he claimed he was born to serve and advise *Aric?*

And now, he was ready to beg forgiveness because a Princesse had chosen to offer him pleasure? Why wouldn't the Princesse chose to offer the fey pleasure?

Staring at him, he asked, "Why?"

Blue gestured to the bed, hardly able to speak. He was weak from the sex, from the rush of magic, from worry. He was bound to Aric, even though the human hadn't realized it, couldn't understand it. If he had displeased Aric…

"Fuck, Blue. I do not own her. I do not own you. And *that* was one of the most erotic things I have ever done in my life. But if you are going to feel fucking guilty, we will not be doing any sort of repeat. Ever," Aric snarled, dropping onto the bed.

Blue felt the relief flood him, and with it, the weariness faded. He set the safeguards around the room so that they would know if somebody tried to disturb them while they slept, then he checked with his kin to see how the plans were going. Ah, good. Even now, the mortals he needed were in route—secretly of course—to Edouine.

"Then I shall banish the guilt. Because the Princesse bade me to tell you tonight she wants the pleasure you teased her with," Blue said with his characteristic smile. He snapped his fingers and the room was restored to rights, the torn gown gone, the other plainer one with the seeds back in the Princesse's room. Off her rather lovely body, of course.

He had worked his fey magic…she would tell the King of the night's events, and remark on her lover's looks, but not his name. The King would not miss the resemblance to his former Master at Arms. Nor would the King be able to strike out in his anger.

Alhdeade had chosen unwisely when he had chosen to strike out at Aric, Blue mused as he lay down on the other side of the bed, while his Master slipped into sleep. Blue was one of the more powerful demi-elves the fey had ever seen. And by the time Blue was done with King Alhdeade, the King was going to wish he had never seen Aric, the half marked Caste.

Chapter Five

Subterfuge

The King's face was blood red with rage. Amery kept her face blank. She was afraid of how he would react. She hadn't told this to Aric, but she was. As she fought to keep from cowering, a now familiar voice slid through her mind, chiding her softly, *"Do you think my Master would allow you to suffer any more? The King will not strike out at you, Princesse Amery, Royal of Edouine."* Upon hearing Blue's voice, the fear faded, and she felt safe — like Blue was there, like Aric was there.

"Since you recall so much of the night, where did this deflowering take place?" Alhdeade demanded.

She shook her head, her hair falling around her shoulders. She made certain she looked suitably shamed and distressed, though her body buzzed with pleasure and joy. "I know not. The servant has wild magicks and I fear he clouded my mind," she said softly. "But tis no dream. I found markings on my body that could only come from a man's touch."

The court physician colored briefly and said humbly, "Her nurse sent for me at the Princesse's request. She has been mated, and deflowered. Her thighs were stained with her virgin's blood and a man's seed."

She felt her lips curve and she kept her head bowed. *If only you knew, physician. There is more seed staining me than just my thighs.* Pressing her lips together, she recalled the way Aric had plundered her from behind while Blue had gripped her hair and driven his shaft deep inside her mouth. It should have choked her, logically there was no way she should have been able to tolerate such a massive length down her throat for so long. Heat puddled low in her belly, her thighs clenched and she fought off the need to moan. It only worsened when Blue's voice whispered in her mind, *"Princesse, are you having sweet memories?"* and she swore she felt the phantom touch of hands caressing her.

Alhdeade's bellow shook the room and Amery was relieved when he ordered her away, but then she pleaded to be allowed to remain. *How can I help protect him if I don't know the King's plan?*

Blue's warm chuckle slid through her mind. *"A true and noble Queen you will be. Perhaps honor can be restored to Edouine. Fear not for my Master, Amery, Princesse Royal. I will listen and learn of what they plan."*

So she fled to her rooms. She was sleeping when her nurse came in and marked her clothing, all of it, with a heavy golden seal of magic, one that would rupture and burst, staining her lover the moment she touched him. Following behind the nurse, cloaked by an invisible shield, Blue smiled lazily, his length hardening underneath his loincloth until it threatened to fall free. Listening to the sweet whispers from Amery's mind were nearly driving him mad. Absently, he cupped his hand over it as he watched the nurse work, which slowly caused his lust to subside—the old crone. If left alone with the Princesse for long, Blue was certain the lust would return. Just the scent of her now was enough to arouse him.

Shortly after the nurse had finished setting the spell into all of the Princesse's clothes she closed and locked the door behind her. The elf moved to the deep dressing chambers and studied the many articles of clothing. He could break the charm, easily and quickly, but why? It would suit his needs well. Aric would briefly be marked by the golden dust, but neither Amery nor he would see it. It would not become visible until he stepped into the morning sun. When the King's men came looking, it would make him stand apart, and they would take him.

Blue studied this with pursed lips and decided it would work well. Of course, Aric was going to feel some heat for a while, and chances were, Amery would be quite angry with him…but once Alhdeade was revealed for the monster he was, and all knew who Aric truly was—yes. This would work well.

The retinue searching for the missing Prince of Amser was rapidly closing in, led by the earl, the Sovereign and the Keeper of the Crown until the Prince was brought home and crowned. Amser had many Seers and they knew he wasn't dead, but he had been missing so long— since his father had taken his foreign mother home so she and the boy could visit her family. The boy was marked by the Royal House of Amser, low on his groin with a half-star, the color, ironically, of Blue's eyes.

The elf smiled and retreated, sending out a call to his kin. They alerted the retinue to make haste, but to travel in silence, while they sent for reinforcement. Not that Alhdeade would dare to attack one from Amser. Amser was nearly three times the size of Edouine, and bred warriors like nothing Edouine had ever seen. No wonder Aric had such a knack for weapons.

Amser kept to itself, simply because that suited Amser. But there was not a country around that would not shudder with fear if Amser were to turn an angry eye its way. Their warriors were strong, brave and bold, men *and* women, having both honor and cunning. They had wizards and healers with magicks almost as powerful as the noble fey.

The country was ripe with grain and herd animals and water and could live unto itself, with no outside interference, or it could trample over any other that dared to stand in its way.

No, Amser was not a power to be trifled with.

And Edouine was going to try to put the missing Prince to death—Aric was going to be royally pissed over that, Blue decided as he slid into sleep once more. He had time for a quick nap before bringing Amery back one more time.

After tonight, the next time Amery and Aric were together, they would be as they should, married and joined, King and Queen, co-rulers of two adjoined lands. Blue grinned sleepily. And he had helped do that—what more could a noble fey ask for?

Chapter Six

Double the Pleasure, Twice the Price

Aric groaned as he felt the smooth silken body slither up his, Amery's mouth covering his as their limbs entwined. "How can you sleep?" she asked, nipping his lip. "We have only the night, Aric. Wake up, already."

He rolled her under him, keeping silent about how he had been working his way through the city and had secured what he needed. The King would receive a deadly draught at his wedding feast. Of course, Aric would most likely be caught. And killed quite horribly, but Amery wouldn't have to suffer a life with that honorless bastard.

Ah, Blue may well be able to save him, but mayhap not. Could one demi-fey battle a King and his wizards?

He sent a thought flying towards Blue and the elf was there, taking his place at the Princesse's breast, cuddling her sweet body as Aric rose and removed his clothing. He moved around the bed and lay down against her back, rubbing and cuddling his cock between the cheeks of her ass. "Are you certain you wish to do this, Amery, love of my heart?" he whispered, as Blue moved down her body. He had taken one ivory thigh in his big ebony hand and was now hungrily laving her clit with his tongue, using his fingers to work her cream backward and lubricate the crevice. "Such an act can be painful at first—"

"Nay," Blue interrupted, pulling his face briefly from her sex to look up at them. "Sex with a fey can be a sweet thing. Any pain she feels I can cloud. She will feel only as much as she desires." A roguish smile slashed his face, wet from her cream. He licked his lips and shuddered. "Such a sweet pussy you have, little Princesse. A little pain can add much pleasure — but the choice is yours."

Amery craned her head and stared at Aric. "I want this, pain or no." She sobbed when she felt Blue's tongue pierce her. Then Aric's finger pierced her ass, slicked with some oily warm substance that smelled of sweet vanilla, hot male, and sex. His teeth bit her shoulder briefly and he said roughly, "Then I shall give it to you. Whatever you ask of me, whenever you ask it, it is yours." He started to pump his finger in and out of her tight rosette, feeling her arch back against him and moan hungrily as he wrapped his other arm around her and cupped her breast, pinching the nipple tightly.

The glove of her ass squeezed him so snug, so hot and silkily that Aric clenched his teeth, driven near insane by it as she shuddered in his embrace. "Always?" she purred, rocking her hips back and forth — back to feel his finger, first one, then two, sliding inside her ass, forward to feel Blue's rather magical tongue inside her cleft.

"Always," he promised mindlessly, probing, stroking, working his two fingers in and out.

She climaxed against them with a scream and Blue rolled on his back, taking her slim body and pulling her atop him, forcing his thick cock deep inside. "Now, Aric, my friend, while she is in the midst of her passion," he said gruffly, hardly aware he had dropped the 'Master'. He shuddered as her tight little sheath gripped his length.

He gritted his teeth, shifted on the bed, spread his wings wider beneath him until he was comfortable.

Aric positioned himself behind her, slicking his cock with the oil until he gleamed with it. Then he smeared it all over Amery's hole while she shuddered and gasped, rocking on Blue's thick cock. Aric prodded the tiny little hole and shuddered, ordering tightly, "Push down."

She was half mindless though. Blue eased inside her mind, took control and did it for her as he slid his ebony hands down her body, grasping her ass and spreading her cheeks, swirling up a tiny bit of fey magic to create a phantom hand to fondle her swollen clit as Aric surged slowly inside. He felt Aric's silent command, *"Do not let me hurt her, Blue,"* and he responded in kind, *"I cannot stop the pain of your entry, but she will not feel it, I swear."* He used his control over her body to pull her to him so he could take her mouth.

He loved the taste of a mortal woman, so fresh and innocent, so sweet. And the Princesse was like a fine wine on his tongue. She hugged his thick cock so tightly, shifting and squirming, her body recognizing the pain, even though he kept her mind from acknowledging it.

Aric stared down at his length as he worked it slowly into the tight chamber of her anal sheath, his chest dripping with sweat, his sac tight, his cock aching with the need to plunder and thrust. She squirmed around him, whimpering mindlessly, rocking against him, "Oh, please, Aric, please. It's not enough—more, I need, I can't oh—" the broken words fell from her lips as he gripped her hips and pushed his shaft deeper inside the tight little hole.

She wailed and pushed back, arching up and taking him inside with a short scream.

Aric pushed down and hissed, "Amery," but Blue had a firm hold on her body and made her bear down, easing the way and she took him inside as he fogged her mind, clouded the pain that tried to snake through and let her feel only that insidiously sweet pain-laced pleasure that so intoxicated.

"Amery," Aric groaned raggedly as she took his cock completely inside, so that his sac swung forward, his pubic curls resting against her sweet ass as she shuddered and rocked hungrily against him.

She collapsed against the black vault of Blue's chest, her red curls tangling with the black of his, her spine arching up, her body shaking and quivering as she rocked mindless back and forth on the shafts that impaled her.

Aric stared down at where he was joined to her, his shaft fully nestled in her ass, the hot satiny walls gripping him so snug and tight that he groaned as he pulled out and pushed back in, feeling Blue mirror his movements in slow tandem as Amery moaned hungrily between them.

Amery felt full, hungry, stretched and dying. She rocked and pleaded as Blue slowly released his hold on her body, his hands sliding from her ass, one going to cup her breast, pushing it up while he lifted his head to take her red nipple deep in his mouth, his pale crystalline eyes staring up at her. His other hand went down to stroke her clit, which was swollen and hard. She was so wet, so slick, and just that light touch gave her a quick orgasm.

Aric groaned as she spasmed around him and he started to plunge. Blue waited until Aric pulled out and then he drove his long cock deep inside so that they moved in synchronization, the elf stroking her sweet swollen little clit, suckling her stiff nipples, while Aric groaned and praised the taut, snug fit of her ass.

Amery wailed as the pressure built again. The hot/cold chills that flooded through her veins robbed her of the ability to think, to see, almost to breathe. She felt nothing beyond the thrusts in her throbbing pussy, in her hot, tightly stuffed ass. The little climax she had received when Blue stroked her clit had been barely a sip and she was dying of thirst.

Throwing her head back, she shoved her hips hard against Aric's, trying to force him deeper inside. "More," she begged weakly, but still Aric moved slowly. Blue smiled and started to drive harder into her and she shuddered. "She is needy, Master, do you deny your love what she craves?" Blue asked roughly, his deep, exotic voice sending shivers down her spine as his breath caressed her wet, tight nipples.

Aric tried to hold back when Amery pushed back harder against him again. *"She will feel no pain, Master. Aric, my friend, the woman is a healer, she knows her body, and I would not allow a woman to suffer at any person's hands, even yours,"* Blue whispered through his mind. That mental voice, usually so easy and smooth, was gruff and strained and hot, full of emotion and need, and the elf's need fired Aric's. Blue showed Aric how Amery was feeling, inside her skin, the need too hot, too large and her body far too small to hold it all inside. Aric's restraint crumbled as he started to shaft that tight little hole heavily, reveling in the short wild screams that filled the air, the shudders that wracked her slim, beautiful body.

Amery screamed, "Yes, yes, harder," reaching up to lace her hands around the posts of the headboard as Aric drove inside. Blue pounded upward, working his long, thick cock completely inside her small snug pussy, growling and swearing in a lyrical foreign tongue, setting his teeth into the fleshy part of her breast and biting down, then laving the faint teeth marks left behind.

Aric pounded harder, feeling his balls draw tight as his orgasm drew near. He lifted his hand and smacked Amery's little ass. She screamed and clenched down on him, coming and squirming, and begging for more all in the same breath. He spanked her again, pulled out and plunged deeply, roughly inside as he shouted out her name, and Blue came. He felt her come again, as he slapped her ass harder, as he fucked the sweet little hole and shoved her down so that she was sandwiched between his body and Blue's.

Blue swore and groaned and roused, driving his still rigid length up and rocking tightly against her, grinding himself against her clit, so that he drew her climax out as Aric started to come, biting down on her shoulder and moaning. He pulled out, burrowed back in and held still, filling her hot little ass with his seed, rocking against her tight butt with short deep hunches of his hips as she milked him dry. Amery was sobbing and whimpering beneath him as her climax wore on, the last of the shudders fading from her body just as he emptied himself inside her.

Aric rolled off of her and pulled her down to cuddle against him. She smiled sleepily at him and said, "I'm a healer, you know. Feed me, let me rest a few minutes and I can make sure we can do this again." Then she slid Blue a hot look and said, "But can we try switching places?"

Chapter Seven

The Revenge

Aric stared at the chains binding him, the faint gold dust that had marked him and shown the guards who had dared to take the noble King's bride. "She's his fucking daughter," Aric had growled as they read off the charges while dragging him through the streets.

Blue had conveniently disappeared. *Where is my faithful servant?* Aric thought, half wildly. He did not so much mind dying; it was dying before he could make sure Amery was not bound to the honorless dog.

He had been sleeping when the door to his room crashed open. He had slept soundly, deeply—Blue had placed such solid safeguards around the room that Aric had not feared discovery.

But the safeguards weren't there. They hadn't failed, they were *gone.* Aric knew the scent and feel of magic, even if he had none of his own. That had been missing. So where had his servant gone, the one who had sworn he was bound to Aric, even unto death? Aric hadn't realized just how attached he had grown to the fey, until the sickening backlash of betrayal swept in to drown him.

"Fear not, my Master, my friend, Aric. I have not deserted you – though I can understand why it must seem so."

Aric jerked so hard his head rapped into the wall and he reached up to rub the tender spot as he swore hoarsely.

He'd been in this hell hole more than a day—a day without food was no true concern, even a day without water was no true hardship. But damn it, his throat was dry. That was the least of his discomforts though. They had wrenched one shoulder when dragging him here, even though he would not fight them, they had not allowed him to walk. He had averted the open-handed slaps that they had thrown to his face, but his belly, ribs, sides and back ached. Few marks, but Aric knew well how easy it was to damage the human body without leaving a single red mark.

He suspected the King had told them not to rough him up too much—too battered and he might elicit sympathy from the crowd that was supposed to hate him.

"Where in the six bloody Hells are you, Blue?"

Blue's laughter filled his mind as he sat in his cell, staring out through the tiny window. *"I am where I can serve you best, my lord, my friend. My King."* And then the voice was gone while Aric demanded to know what the hell Blue was talking about.

"Look, you winged black creature, noble fey, one boon I ask of you. Damn it, answer me!"

A rustling sigh filled the room and Blue was there, not in body, but in the flickering blue light which Aric snatched out of the air and cupped in his palm. "Amery...she deserves more than to be wed to that bloody bastard. He is not worthy. Judge him, cast upon him what he deserves, and give her what she deserves," he whispered, hearing a guard moving down the hall.

"Easily will I grant that wish, even if you had not asked, my Master, Aric my friend," Blue said, his deep voice echoing through Aric's mind, the blue light spinning

rapidly in his hands before disappearing in a tiny puff of smoke.

Aric sagged in relief, pulling his long braid over his shoulder, propping his back against the wall, and falling into a weary sleep. All in all, even if he died tomorrow, he had gotten in life what he had asked for—he had loved Amery, had served and saved his country, and Amery would be free from Alhdeade.

He was roused, briefly, from his sound sleep by Blue's chiding mental voice, like a hand squeezing his shoulder.

"As I have said once already, fear not. You will not be dying today, tomorrow, or any time soon."

* * * * *

He shifted, pulling against the steel cuffs that bound him. The judges stared while the hot sun pounded down on him. They had stripped him down to a white loin cloth, and he knew they sought to humiliate him. Glaring insolently up at the Tribunal, he kept his shoulders back, and let them know they had failed. He wasn't broken or even weakened by the lack of food or water for a day—it would take more than that.

Bloody hell, he had forced his men to suffer at least that before he would even take them on in training for the Royal Army. One day and night was nothing.

Women stared at his long, lean warrior's body and hungered. Men eyed him with jealousy, or saw the pride and easy confidence in his gaze and looked away. A man with honor did not act without honor as they said this one had.

"You raped the King's bride," they accused.

He smirked. "I loved her," he countered.

"You treated her like a scullery maid," they accused.

"At first. I was angry with her father. The King threw me out after many years of loyal service, and left me to die on the road after I had *saved* his entire army from slaughter at the hands of the Akkerites. I am the Master at Arms, Aric the half-marked Caste. I bear the scar I took at the battle saving his life. He knows this to be true," he said, nodding at the King who glared at him in rage. "You know it to be true. All of you know my name. He thought I would die and never be able to tell what happened in those days or else he would have certainly killed me.

"But I lived," Aric said heatedly. "I took my anger out on Amery, the Princesse Royal. I dishonored myself and her, and for that I beg her forgiveness. Her forgiveness, not his. He is a man without honor. She is his child in all *but blood*. He raised her at her mother's, the Queen Royal Halah's side since she was but an infant. You all know this to be true and none have the honor or courage to say it."

"Cease your tongue's wagging," one of the Tribunals judge's hissed, beckoning for one of the gallows's men to take Aric. "You will die for your crimes."

A high Caste earl moved out from one of the turrets surrounding the castle, staring down into the crowd. "Hold. I am the Queen's cousin, the Princesse Royal's cousin. As her blood kin, even without the King's approval, I have the right to speak for this man who claims to have her love —"

"He is unmarked —"

"No. He has a half mark and he is a lord. His Caste is unknown to us, but he did save Edouine, the King himself decreed it so," Earl Rigmond said softly, staring down. He had intense, brooding eyes that saw clear through the greed and malice on the faces of the Tribunal judges. He stared down at Aric and smiled slightly at him before glancing at his men and nodding.

His guards moved out of the crowd to surround Aric. Aric's eyes widened at this rather unexpected development.

And he heard a soft chuckle in his mind. "*So Edouine is not without honor, even without you in it, my Master and friend,*" Blue said quietly. "*But all is well, even without the high Caste earl. You have unknown friends coming. And the earl shall pass judgment.*"

"He will die for his crimes," the King bellowed.

Rigmond narrowed his eyes and demanded, "What crimes? Bedding the Princesse? Not a death crime, that, unless her blood kin decree. If it were rape, he would die. But was it rape?"

"I've voiced my disgust over your union with the Princesse Royal and none have heard me. I've been refused audience with my own cousin and now I will insist. But first — this. What crimes? Bedding the Princesse? Again I say, that is not a crime worthy of death unless her blood kin decree." Rigmond smiled evilly. "You've decreed you are not her blood kin so that you may wed and bed her. Therefore, that is my duty. And I say...why should he die? He has begged forgiveness for any trespass against the Princesse Royal and I will speak with Amery. Any punishment she sees fit, I will mete out and —"

The King bellowed, "Kill him!"

Aric flung up his arms to ward off the arrows, but none came. Blue arrived in a whirlwind of fire and smoke, along with more than fifty black clad riders, bearing the Royal insignia of Amser. The arrows couldn't breach the wall of fire and the guards loyal to the King knocked more arrows to set loose but before Aric's eyes could clear from the smoke he was surrounded by men he had never seen — clad in black velvet, black chain mail — who offered him their backs and their shields, keeping any and all attackers away.

But not one attacker dared come. Aric knew of Amser.

Not one of his men would want to face a knight of Amser. *Ten* Edouinites wouldn't want to face a knight of Amser, Aric suspected.

But why were they protecting him?

"I told them to stop coming in secret. Alhdeade would not dare assassinate so many of them, and none from Amser," Blue said with a laugh as the arrows fell broken to the ground. *"Amser would rain down fire on his House and he would die before he knew why he was dying."*

Aric was silent, staring in confusion at the odd insignia on the shields and head-guards. A half-star, blue, surrounded by a circle, with a sword and spear crossing through. The half-star...just like his own.

A man threw one leg over the back of a magnificent horse. "Who dares to assault a Prince Royal from the House of Amser?" he demanded in a deep, rolling and familiar voice. Aric's ears pricked and he was flung back in time, hearing that same voice.

Hands, big and strong, scarred but loving..."He looks like me, not his father, thanks to the Goddess. Your Royal mother should be glad of that...but you will have your father's Crown and your mother's wits..."

"My boy...oh, Aric, look...there they go, your father and his brother...hunting again. They'll be taking you with them soon."

Aric's head was spinning. The man moving across the courtyard toward him looked familiar and he felt the years falling away. The circle of men protecting him parted for the man, then closed instantly around them, and they were enclosed by an unyielding wall of knights.

He *knew* this man. "You used to be so much larger," he murmured, shaking his head. "Who are you?"

The man smiled, his weathered face glowing. "You used to be so much smaller, my Prince, my liege Lord. I am Telcan Dule, your uncle, the Sovereign Ruler of Amser until you come home. But first..." He turned, staring up at the Tribunal. In a deep, booming voice, he said, "Amser has business to attend to with Edouine. Will we do so here, in public?"

* * * * *

The advisers of Edouine didn't understand why the Sovereign insisted the half marked Caste be brought before the advisors on whatever business Amser had to discuss with Edouine. Or why they insisted he be allowed to be taken by the Amser retinue and dressed. But when he came striding out in front of them...dressed in a black doublet, his black hair flowing down his back, Blue at his side — wearing trousers, for once, his wings spread wide at his back — the advisors of Edouine started to worry.

The Tribunal, many of them also advisors, had wanted to scatter, but Alhdeade had forbidden it, and now they whispered and wondered and worried amongst themselves.

What really bothered them was the gold coronet at Aric's brow. In the center gleamed a blue jewel, shaped like a half-star.

Blue at his left, the Sovereign at his right, Aric stood before the Tribunal and the King, an insolent smirk on his face. He had just received a crash course, courtesy of fey magic in Royal politics, and he had been insulted greatly. The mark on his groin would have been recognized, if any had taken the time to look. His former Master, the previous Master at Arms should have recognized it. So the injuries done to Aric went back decades, not just a few years.

The mark wasn't a Caste mark. It was the mark of the Royal House of Amser. Amser had no Caste system. Amser felt it was brutish and senseless that a person could work all their life and never rise above a scullery maid. You couldn't work your way into the Royal House, but you could rise far in Amser, if you so chose. A child born to a whore didn't have to grow up to be a whore — in fact, the child born to a whore was carefully watched, and if not cared for properly, the child was taken and given to those who loved and wanted it. And even the whores in Amser were treated better than some of the highest servants in Edouine.

"I believe, Telcan, you have some explaining to do," Alhdeade said, sitting on his throne, staring at Aric with eyes that glittered with rage.

"I suggest," Blue said silkily, "you address the Sovereign with the title he is due. Amser has been insulted. Do not make things worse."

"Do not speak to me, you vile creature of the night!" Alhdeade spat.

Blue smiled slowly. "I am no servant nor citizen nor denizen of this country. I may speak to whomever I choose. I know the laws of the land as well as you, but the fey do not live by human laws. The fey do not harm the humans. You brought this on yourself, Alhdeade—remember the tiny little noble fey? The one your men toyed with, the one you told Aric to kill? If you had but cared about the harm your men brought, the luck would have been in part yours," Blue said.

Alhdeade's mouth opened, but one of his advisors, apparently one of the few blessed with a mind, spoke in a quick whisper, and Alhdeade clamped his mouth closed. "Whatever ills my men brought upon your kin, I beg forgiveness. But that has nothing to do with what has happened in Edouine. Leave us, noble fey."

Blue laughed and every man and woman in the room shuddered as though he had rubbed their spines with a velvet glove—all but Aric. His deep, rolling voice had little effect on the one he called friend. "Leave?" he mocked lightly. "Leave, you say? I cannot leave. Aric, Master at Arms, is my Master. I am demi-fey. For me to leave him is to go to my death."

Some of the more learned ones paled. The demi-fey only bonded once, and it was a deep bond, as deep a bond as that of a soul-mate bond. Alhdeade turned gray. To kill Aric would be to kill Blue. And you did not kill the noble fey...not so blatantly as that. A tiny little smoke elf was so easily done, but this massive creature that towered over everyone in the room?

"Your Master has dishonored the Princesse, the King's chosen bride," one of the advisors said, stepping forward. "What would be a just punishment?"

Telcan chose at the moment to step forward. "What is the just punishment for the King who threw aside the man to whom this country owes its very life?" he asked. "What is the just punishment for the King who has forced the Princesse Royal into an unwanted marriage? What is the just punishment for the King who has used malice and murder and evil doing to force that Princesse into that marriage? What is the just punishment for the King who would have killed the Prince Royal of Amser? The Prince loves the Princesse — bedding his love is no *crime.*"

"He is no Prince!" Alhdeade roared, surging from his throne and throwing his arm in Aric's direction.

In response, Telcan brushed aside his doublet and the under shirt, rolling down his breeches just enough to bare the mark, the blue half-star, the mark of the Royal House of Amser that all children born into the line bore. "You recognize the mark, do you not, Alhdeade?" Telcan asked, dropping the title as Alhdeade had dropped his.

Recognizing at last the unsteady ground he walked, Alhdeade said, "Yes, Sovereign. I know well that mark of Amser."

He turned gray when Aric revealed his own mark, his pale green eyes flashing insolently as he stared at the King before adjusting his clothes. "I remember Telcan, well. I thought of him often, though I did not remember his name. I remember the carriage ride and my parents, but not their names. But your citizens who found me were Caste lords and ladies...one of them should have known this mark.

"I served you proudly and loyally for years, and you left me to die," Aric said, moving forward, away from the men of Amser and Blue. "I saved Edouine and we both know I could have used that wish to take what I desired above all else, the Princesse Royal. Instead I used it to save your people and the reward I received was a death sentence."

"But I did not die. The woman who gave me water and food and healing was a witch and I spent many weeks doing her slave work, including fetching a blue light from down a well," he said, flashing Blue a quick grin. "So perhaps I should thank you." I found my Royal Adviseur and Council that grim day, and the means to repay you.

"I fully intended to come back here and treat the Princesse cruelly, like a servant, the way you treated me, nothing more. But seeing her, I wanted her, remembered how much I had always loved her. I was still angry, but my desire for her and desire for vengeance overwhelmed all else. I took her—but it was not rape, Alhdeade." He smiled, a hot male smile as he whispered for Alhdeade only, "You know it was not rape, and you knew it then. That is why you wanted me dead—and you knew it was me that first night, didn't you?"

"You're a bloody fucking criminal," Alhdeade rasped, Royal manners falling aside in his rage. But things had changed and he knew he could not strike the man in front of him, nor draw his sword and order his men to hold him while he chopped off his penis and fed it to him. "It was rape and theft."

Rigmond's voice interrupted. "That's the first thing we will resolve," he said as he moved to the dais. "The Princesse Royal Amery approaches gentlemen, and you will remember how to conduct yourselves with a lady present," he warned, glaring at Alhdeade. "King you may be, for now, but I am her blood kin and that gives me some rights that even you cannot supercede."

"The bastard fucking raped her! He stole my bride and he and that perverted elf molested and assaulted—"

Amery's warm, golden laughter spilled through the throne room. "*Ah, my Master, your love is a wondrous sight,*"

Blue mused as they turned to admire the Princesse. She moved into the room, attendants at her side, the fading bruise still on her cheek.

"Rape? Why, how can it be rape? I had only pleasure at their hands—at yours, I had only pain and suffering and bruising," she said, reaching up to touch the mark on her lovely face. Half of her curls were caught up and woven through a coronet of pearls, the rest spilled down her back in a wild cascade. She wore simple drops in her ears. "Assaulted? No assault, unless you want to say my senses were assaulted by overwhelming pleasure. Or I could spout poetical, lyrical phrases and say my heart was assaulted by the overwhelming love I have always felt for the handsome Master at Arms, Aric, who is no longer the Half Marked Caste. Or the Master at Arms, actually, for the King, my *step-father*, threw him aside when he should have lifted him up and thanked him."

She crossed the throne room and as she moved, men and women bowed or curtsied before her. She paused beside Blue and he went to one knee and crossed one hand over his heart before offering her his other. She accepted and he lifted her hand to his lips, turning it and pressing a kiss to her wrist. She dipped in a tiny curtsy and narrowed her eyes at him. He arched a brow in acknowledgement of her words, *"You will pay for the suffering he endured, Blue. Fond of you as I am, you will pay."*

He didn't tell her that he had. Every wound that had been inflicted on Aric he had felt, and every moment that Aric had hungered and suffered Blue had done the same. The Princesse wouldn't understand exactly what his bond to the Prince Royal was—not even the Prince did. But Blue would take whatever she felt she must give him, for he hated that Aric must suffer at all, even though he had known exactly how this would turn out.

After Blue released her she lowered her head and pressed a kiss to his ebony brow, caressing the silky locks long enough to have Alhdeade's hands clenching in rage, and then she lifted her head to smile serenely at him, thinking just how long he had made *her* suffer.

"*Go on, now, Princesse,*" Blue chided softly, an unseen hand low on her spine. Even that very casual touch made her shudder minutely. "*Your Prince is waiting.*"

"No rape, Father mine," she said, mocking Alhdeade. "No rape at all. I was loved, good and well. Outside the bonds of marriage, perhaps, but there's no harm in that, you see. I've already spoken with my Lord Uncle and explained the duress I was under when I was forced to accept your proposal. And he will not allow the marriage, will you, my Lord Uncle?"

Rigmond smiled fondly down at Amery, stroking a weathered hand over her red curls. "No, child of my cousin, blood of my blood, I will not allow that. And as our laws decree, that is my right." He slid Alhdeade a narrow look, his eyes sparking with his anger. "You think that because you denied me access to my cousin I knew nothing of her unhappiness, of her abuse? That sham of a marriage would never have happened, Alhdeade, but now—now at least I know my cousin shall find happiness in the arms of her husband."

With that, he led her to Aric, while Alhdeade gaped at them with shock, then he started to tremble with rage. "No," he rasped. "I'll not have it." He started to lunge, but before he could several things happened.

Aric moved, drawing the sword from his back and placing Amery behind him, where his knights gathered protectively around her. Blue moved between Aric and Alhdeade and the men who still saw Alhdeade as King.

"What are you doing?" Alhdeade rasped as Blue moved closer.

Alhdeade could not move. His hands flexed convulsively as he tried to draw his sword, but he was frozen. The look on Blue's handsome, alien face was terrible—cold and beautiful, the look of justice and death. "Judgment," Blue replied softly. "The noble fey were given unto this land eons ago as its caretakers. You slaughtered innocents to coerce the Princesse into marriage, you left your faithful servant to die. He did not die, but that is not because you did not try. And you suspected, I think, all along that he was of noble blood. The least of your crimes, true, but then you would have killed him. And to kill a Prince is a wicked thing—to kill an innocent man, a terrible thing."

Alhdeade was having trouble breathing. As Blue's face grew closer and closer, the elf whispered huskily, "Judgment."

* * * * *

Aric stared out the window, at the rolling green fields and felt something inside his heart stir. This was home.

Behind him he heard nothing, but he knew Blue was there. "Why are you going?"

Blue laughed. "It's stronger. I said nothing, and you knew I was here. And you know I plan to leave."

Turning, Aric cocked a brow and waited. Blue smiled, a flash of white in his dark face. "You need to be alone with her for your wedding night and the honeymoon," Blue said, lifting one massive shoulder. "I'll not be far."

"You suffer when not near me. And you felt every blow I took, and thirsted and hungered the day and night with me. How deep does this bond go?"

Blue lifted his pale eyes to study Aric. "I've never had a bond with a mortal, so I know not. In time, you will learn to guard your thoughts from me, and you will learn to speak into my mind as clearly as I can speak into yours. You will feel my emotions and thoughts as clearly as I feel yours. Beyond that..." Blue spread his hands and his wings wide. "I will never betray you. I am your friend, your companion, your brother in our souls. I am here to help however I can. There are things coming that you must need me for or else I would have been sent to another, Aric."

"What of Amery?"

"I guard her with my life. She is your lady wife and I honor and cherish her as I honor and cherish you," Blue said simply.

"That is not exactly what I meant," Aric said, running a hand through his hair. *Blast it all. When does the fucking sun set here?* Amser tradition said he went to his bride on their wedding night at sundown.

"What did you mean?"

"I am not certain," Aric said, pacing the room. He wanted Amery. Fuck. His skin felt too tight. He was edgy, hungry and needy. And he was trying to talk about something important with the one other person in his life who mattered. *Not wise, not wise at all, Aric,* he told himself. "How do I explain this?" he muttered. "I love her. In all my life, she is *all* I have ever loved. So why do I feel as though it is right that I share her with you?"

Blue's eyes and face went blank.

"I am not saying that every time I touch her I want it to be with you there, but I also do not see what we shared before as never happening again," Aric whispered harshly, staring at Blue. "And neither does Amery. She is in love with me. In her heart and in her soul she is mine. But she is drawn to you. And now I ask you again, what of Amery? She will want it often, if I know the lady well. And I want her to have all that she desires. Have you any desire to take a wife of your own? Will our needs cause you pain?"

Blue's familiar laugh filled the air. "You do not understand this, truly, Aric. Your needs and mine are one," Blue said. "You remain yourself, yes. As will I. But many things will become as one. Your most basic instincts will shape and form mine…as I truly, until now, have had none. I've no desire to take a mate in life. What would pain me would be to never know the touch of your lady wife's body again…but I would accept that, if knowing that taking of it caused you pain.

"So you ask me, what of Amery? I tell you, I will cherish and adore her, *as you do.* But she is your lady."

And Blue would do what Aric wished. "Share our bed? Only? Amery—"

Aric felt Blue rush gently into his mind, felt the larger man's hands land on his shoulders as he spoke, realizing how much Aric had inside that he couldn't put into words. *"You have need of Amery only — Amery is all I will have need of. As often, or as little as you do. Stop torturing yourself Aric, and do not trouble your mind—"*

"How can I not?" Aric rasped. "I'm allowing another man to fuck my wife—I should have problems with that. Why do I not? And I am not just talking about when I am with you, Blue. I will often have to leave and I will leave you here with her, to protect and care for her, and that is part of it. I'm giving another man leave to fuck my wife. Why is that not a problem?"

Blue shrugged and asked softly, "Why does it matter? But let me explain it thus—"*Not another man, but a mirror. The other half of the same coin, you and I. We are a matched pair, which is why Amery is drawn to me and is how you found me. You passed by four other houses on the way to the witch, know you that, Aric?*"

And then Blue was gone.

But not too far, as promised.

Chapter Eight

The Wedding Night

Aric moved up the stairs, leaving behind the loud, boisterous crowd. Amser was indeed grateful to have their Prince back. In three days time, he would be King. But he had wanted his bride first and the Sovereign had allowed it.

He took the steps up the tower, the light growing dim, lit only by the sconces on the wall. He was so hard he ached with it.

There was no door. The only door to the bridal bower was at the foot of the stairs, which he had locked behind him and kept the key. No one in, no one out. A remnant from when Amser had been more barbarian than civilized, and the brides had often tried to flee before being bedded. It also kept any merrymakers from coming in on them.

He stood in the open arch of the doorway and stared.

Amery was clad in a sheer nightgown that hid nothing—not the fullness of her breasts, her slim torso, the dip of her waist, not the plump lips of her sex, nor the red curls that covered it. Her hair was piled on top of her head in loose, fat curls that would take barely one tug to come falling down.

Aric moved slowly to her, a small smile on his lips as he walked around her. She made a move to cover herself and stopped, a frustrated noise coming from her throat.

"This gown is pointless," she said, her cheeks flushing. "Why wear it?"

Aric trailed one lone finger between the cheeks of her ass, the silky sheer cloth sliding over her sensitive flesh and making her shiver. "To tempt me. To tempt you," he responded as he completed his slow circle. "Lie down." He nodded to the bridal bed as he unlaced the silk shirt he wore and removed his thick leather belt, tossing them aside. He had already kicked his soft, cloth shoes aside downstairs and now wore only the loose black cotton trousers as he lay down between her thighs and pressed the sheer cloth to her cleft, stroking her through it, listening as she cried out. Then he pressed his mouth to her and started to lick and suckle against her clit. The cloth was so sheer he could press his tongue against it and enter her wet slit.

When she was riding his mouth, he moved back, replacing his mouth with his hand and pulling the long fall of his hair away when she sobbed and reached for him. "Not so quickly, Princesse mine," he teased. "This is a night I never thought to have. I want it to last."

"Aric," she whimpered, rocking her hips up, her head thrashing on the pillow. The carefully arranged curls had fallen free and lay tumbled around her shoulders, spilling over her breasts, plainly showing through the gossamer of the nightgown. It lay smoothly against her body everywhere but where Aric touched her between her thighs, and there it clung, damp with the cream of her arousal as he stroked her clit. He started to press against her, and the silky, sheer cloth of the gown entered her around his invading fingers, rasping her sensitive swollen tissues.

Aric stared down at her hungrily as he drove first one thick finger inside her wet pussy, then two, staring at her flushed face, her deep blue eyes dazed, hot and heavy. Her nipples were tight and hard, moving in rapid heavy pants as she struggled to breathe. With a growl, he reached for the neckline of the gown and tore it from her body, the fine cloth shredding in his big hand. He pulled his fingers from her clinging tissues and licked the cream from them greedily before he rose and tore his breeches away.

He mounted her, spreading her thighs and catching her mouth with his, sucking her tongue into his mouth as he slid the fat head of his cock against her clit. As she lay under him she began rocking against his body and clutching at him. He took his shaft in one hand and started to enter her, closing his eyes, but he froze when she whispered, "Summon Blue."

A cold chill raced down his spine. It was one thing for him to share her at other times, but not his wedding night. "No," he said, pain settling in his gut.

"Yes. He was supposed to protect and care for you," she said, pressing her hands against his chest, enough for him to know she wouldn't accept him until he did as she asked. "And he allowed you to be harmed. I told him he would pay — and I intend to see it done. You'd never allow me to have him harmed and I could never order it done anyway, so I'll do it this way. I will not deny I yearn to feel what I felt when I lay with you both, and in time, I will take that pleasure again. But it will be a long time, for I intend to make him suffer."

"Summon him, or I'll not let you touch me tonight."

Aric's eyes narrowed and he shifted, moved and pinned her. "You do not have the right to deny me my wedding night," he whispered roughly. There was an ache in his heart, but it was rather bittersweet. She thought she was defending him. Rolling from her, he moved his back to the headboard and stared into the fire across the room. "Blue suffered every blow I took, as though he was being struck the same as me. He suffered every hour I went without water, suffered as they dragged me through the streets and refused me the dignity of walking on my own feet, or even the dignity of relieving myself in private. While he was not there in body, he was there in spirit, for Blue is inside me. What is done to me is done to him."

He pulled his eyes away from the fire and stared at Amery. "I will not summon him here to let you taunt him with your lovely body, wife of mine," he said quietly. "I realize you are angry, but you do not understand what is between Blue and me. Bloody hell, *I* do not fully understand, but I will not allow you to torment him."

"You were tortured and beaten," she hissed, pulling her knees to her chest, not realizing it exposed the folds of her sex in a rather tempting manner.

Aric swallowed the hungry moan that rose in his throat at the sight of her wet, open cleft so sweetly displayed. With a very strong act of will, he dragged his eyes from her slit to her face and stared into her dark, angry eyes. "I was not tortured. And that hardly qualifies as a beating. Blue would not have allowed me to be hurt too badly. Amery, he is loyal, and he knew he had to let it play out as it did—bloody hell, my lady, he was leading the knights and Sovereign into Edouine. Would you prefer he had stayed by my side and I had never known who I am?"

She pouted, poking her lip out.

Arching a black brow at her, Aric drawled, "Perhaps I should explain it this way. What is done to me is done to

Blue. And what is done to Blue is done to me. I suffered. He suffered. If you try to make him suffer, I will suffer. Blue and I are connected, Amery, bonded in the soul. We're a matched pair, he and I." He rolled onto his knees and crawled across the lake-sized bed to her, putting his face to hers, catching her succulent lower lip between his teeth, tugging on it. "And it's cruel of you to ask that I share my wedding night…no matter how angry you may be."

A slow shudder wracked her body and her lids drifted closed. She forced them open and stared up him. "You were hurt," she whispered stubbornly.

Rakishly, he grinned at her while trailing one hand down the side of her bent knee, sliding down under until, he could plunge two fingers inside the prettily exposed slit. "Just a little, and look where it got me, love. You ought to be thanking him," he suggested as he started to pump his fingers in and out. He crowded over her until she fell backward and then he pushed her knees over to one side, keeping them together.

"I'm not sharing my bride in any way on my wedding night," he said gruffly, moving up and prodding her with his cock. The position, with her knees together, kept her closed tightly and he had to work his cock in slowly. "And I'd rather be beaten again, ten times worse, than share you—even with Blue—on this night."

Her eyes flew open as he gripped her, one hand on her ass, the other on her thigh and drove deep inside. Seeing the intent look on his face she gasped, "I am sorry," as he pounded repeatedly into her, marking her, bending over her and filling her tight little sheath with short deep digs. His face was grim, eyes slitted and hungry, the muscles in his chest and belly working as he shafted her with those short, forceful digs that soon brought hungry, whimpering cries to her lips.

Her nipples stood up red and swollen and her torso moved as she gasped in air anxiously, staring up into his face with rapt attention.

He lowered his body over hers and growled as she started to tightened around his cock, the wet creamy heat of her sex caressing his length as he drove back inside.

"Mine," he growled, taking her mouth, biting her lip, thrusting his tongue deep inside. "Mine," he repeated as he kissed and bit his way down her neck. His cock stretched her, filled her. She shifted and squirmed, then screamed when he slid one hand under her thigh and stroked her swollen clit.

"Say it, Amery, say it," he told her as he drove his cock inside her, reveling in the tight silky way her pussy gloved him. Her cream coated him, the scent of it filled the air, and the sweet taste of it still lingered on his tongue. "Say it," he told her as he circled her clit. With his other hand, he found the tight little rosette of her ass and he pushed there, listening with hot satisfaction as she mewled while she tightened around him, her body surging spasmodically as she neared climax.

"Yours," she sobbed. "I swear I am yours."

He spread her thighs, keeping his weight on his hands as he pressed her into the mattress and fucked her harder, roaring out her name as she came, her release triggering his own so that he came in hot pulsing tidal waves that left him weak and shaking.

* * * * *

Blue lay in his bed, half propped on his side, his wings spread wide and fanning the air rapidly in his excitement. Sweat glistened on his long, muscled body as his hand rhythmically pumped his cock. But it wasn't his hand he felt—it was Amery's pussy.

He felt her startlement when she opened her eyes and saw his reflection in Aric's eyes as the men both came at once, Aric into Amery's body, Blue onto his own hand and the fine linens. Aric soothed his lady wife, crooning softly to her and stroking her back, while Blue whispered into her mind, *"I am his, as well. What he feels, I feel."*

Through Aric's eyes he could see the charming blush that pinkened her cheeks.

He knew the moment she understood, felt the realization slam into her. His body still felt the slight aches from the beating. He had soothed Aric's away, but hadn't bothered with his own. Aric probably had not really noticed, but he never should have suffered them. They bothered Blue little—why waste the magic?

"I am sorry, Blue," she whispered from miles away, cuddling into Aric's chest.

"There is no need."

She smiled. He could feel the echo of it, the movement of it through his bond with his mortal. "There is. And I will show you how sorry when you return."

He smiled then, as hot anticipation started to race through his body.

THE END

144

About the author:

Shiloh was born in Kentucky and has been reading avidly since she was six. At twelve, she discovered how much fun it was to write when she took a book that didn't end the way she had wanted it to and rewrote the ending. She's been writing ever since.

Shiloh now lives in southern Indiana with her husband and two children. Between her job, her two adorable and demanding children, and equally adorable and demanding husband, she crams writing in between studying and reading and sleeps when time allows.

Shiloh welcomes mail from readers. You can write to her c/o Ellora's Cave Publishing at P.O. Box 787, Hudson, Ohio 44236-0787.

Also by Shiloh Walker:

Her Best Friend's Lover
The Dragon's Warrior
The Hunter's 1: Declan and Tori
Voyeur
Whipped Cream and Handcuffs

Spell of the Chameleon

By Titania Ladley

Chapter One

It was time to reverse the spell.

Though she wasn't sure why her past condemner's existence had suddenly become a priority, Mia Foxe shifted and kicked her motorcycle into gear. The hum of the motor soothed her, while a chilly October breeze plastered her black leather jacket and pants to her lithe body. The Massachusetts countryside was alive with flavor. As she sped along, she lifted her chin and inhaled the mixed aroma of burning leaves, apple cider, freshly cut wood...and him.

Yes. The scent of him was growing stronger. And the site of Perish, a town that had thrived back in the early 1690s, was just around the next bend.

As was the man whom she'd sentenced to live out eternity alone in the now desolate ghost town.

Downshifting, she found the entrance to the lane where its overgrown foliage presented a wall of bright fall colors. She braked with ease, swinging the bike across the blacktop and moved toward the overgrown trail hidden within the dense brush. Peering through the clear shield of her helmet, Mia studied the many worn signs that had been placed on either side of the old country lane hundreds of years ago by spooked residents who'd abandoned Perish.

Warning! Do not enter! one read.

Another tipped precariously, its wood all but rotten, read, *Witch's territory. If you enter, you die!*

The next elicited a throaty laugh from her. *Evil spirits reside here.*

Oh, yes. Abraham Warwick, the town cleric, had definitely been evil. But she'd shown him who could be the craftier one.

Without flinching, she revved the motor and shot through the branches that impeded outsiders from entering the area encompassed by the spell's curse. The lane dwindled into a narrow path of weeds surrounded by thick forest. Undaunted, she urged the motorcycle through the towering pines and oaks, until shadows gave way to the blinding light of the afternoon sun.

The village, tucked against a soaring cliff, was just as she'd left it over three hundred years ago—a general store, an inn and restaurant, stables, a blacksmith and carpenter, tiny Cape Cod homes with clapboard roofs, English wigwams...and his church. It was exactly the same, except for the absence of people. They'd been affected by her curse. Subtle nuances had been imbedded in their minds to urge them to flee, to leave and never return.

And they had all abandoned the settlement—except Abraham. He'd been imprisoned in Perish to...well, she thought wickedly, to *perish* in his own solitary, eternal insanity.

"Well, well, well." The voice was none other than his, of course. There was no mistaking that deep timbre, a voice which still held remnants of an English accent. "The witch has, at last, returned to stir her boiling cauldron once more. To what do I owe this grand visit?"

Mia swung her gaze to the left, and the sight that met her eyes was one of pure heaven. He was naked! Never in the last several centuries had she ever pondered what this man would have looked like beneath his preacher's robe. In fact, she'd not thought of him again until the recent urge to return to Perish had suddenly gripped her. Now she knew why. Her gaze blazed a trail from the long sandy hair, down over the wide shoulders and solid chest. He was taller than she remembered. And longer, too, she thought, as she moved her stare down the rippling abdomen to the length of his flaccid penis. Oh, she'd never actually *seen* it before for comparison, she silently conceded, but wouldn't her Chameleon senses have known there was a usable tool of perfection attached to the hateful man?

"Shame on you," he snarled.

Mia experienced a rush of blue fire from the depth of her eyes, down to her very toenails. A sweet ache flooded her feminine lips where they sat nestled within the leather of her garment. She watched, awed, as his sex thickened and began to rise.

"No. Shame on *you*," she threw back. "You're the one who's nude—and sporting a growing cock. And here I'd gone all these centuries and thought you to be a eunuch."

He moved one threatening step closer. His fists clenched, as did his pearly white teeth. She could all but see the steam shooting from his nostrils. His magnificent body flexed with each animalistic motion of his limbs, each breath he took. And she thought of a mighty dragon breathing his fire and wrath for all to see.

"Woman..." he began with a warning tone. Clearly restraining himself from attacking her, he stopped in his tracks. Through clamped teeth, he said, "State your reason for returning to taunt me, or else I cannot be held accountable for my actions."

Mia inhaled the rugged scent of him, the caged beast stalking his prey, expression contorted with pure hatred. He was a giant to be feared, to heed. Fearless, she crossed her arms and looked up into the deep chocolate brown of his eyes.

She shrugged. "I don't know why I've come."

His sandy brows arched mockingly. "You don't know why you've come?" he echoed.

"No," she replied, cutting the engine. She swung a leg over the bike and removed her helmet. With a shake of her head, she released her hair, its thick mass tumbling to her shoulders. Purposefully, she stood before him and sat the helmet upon the cushioned seat. "I haven't a clue."

She thought she heard him growl before he replied, "You condemned me to live in a solitary hell with naught but myself for company for well over three centuries, and you haven't a clue why you've suddenly come to remind me of what a witch you truly are?"

"Witch, Abraham? Or bitch?"

His eyes, dark as sin, twinkled for the briefest moment. "Must I choose?"

Age-old simmering anger bubbled from deep within her soul. She stepped so close to him that her leather-clad breasts brushed against his upper abdomen. Ignoring the traitorous tingle of her suddenly taut nipples, she tipped her head back and looked up into the mocking sneer of his beautiful face.

"You chose once, dear Abe." She narrowed her eyes and ducked her head to nip one of his nipples between her teeth. He flinched, but did not move away from her. "You called me witch. You swore to burn my wicked soul at the stake. You sought to banish me to hell, to *murder* me, though I caused no mischief in your precious village of Perish."

"And a witch, you were, as evidenced by your cruel spell." His arms went around her, and she was slammed up against his hard chest. "But before that, you seduced with the sway of your hips," he swiped his hands over her buttocks, "enticed with your shameless deep cleavage." With that, he dipped his head and speared his tongue into the deep valley between her breasts. "By one bat of the eye, you cast spell upon spell over the men—and, yes, even the women—of my town."

Her head fell back. A cauldron's heat scorched her wherever he touched, wherever his eyes brushed her flesh, wherever his hot breath caressed her skin. Her pulse thrummed in her throat like the erratic beat of a drum. With her chest pressed against his unyielding one, she couldn't breathe, couldn't think.

But suddenly, neither did she want to.

"By my mere beauty," she said breathlessly, "I'm banished to die by fire? You call this a fair trial—nay, a trial at all?"

"Trial?" he replied softly. "You didn't stay long enough for that." Swiftly, skillfully, he plunged his hand down the back of her pants.

"No!"

"Yes." He smiled wickedly. Before she could leap from his grasp, or throw up a boundary of protective magic, she felt his grip close over her *trifed*, a battery of sorts, which fed all Chameleons' ability to perform witchcraft. With an adeptness born of a sorcerer, Abe yanked the *trifed* from its place just above her tailbone.

"No…" She choked it out and looked up into his eyes. There, by the light of a brilliant fall day, she swore she saw the epitome of her archrival in his face, the spawn of the devil himself. An odd dizziness washed over her, and her arms went around his waist for support. But she was falling, sliding down his mammoth body as Perish spun around her in a plethora of colors.

"How…did you know…about my *trifed*? Why…why…did you…do this to me?" she hissed.

The last thing she heard before blackness engulfed her was his hate-laced response. "That's precisely the very same question that's been haunting me for over three hundred fucking years!"

* * * * *

Abe gathered her into his arms.

He could still recall the changing colors of her eyes. Like a reptile, they changed with her moods, grass green with humor, red with anger, black as the hate boiled in her soul, and sparkling blue with deep passion and emotion. As he carried her to the inn, he studied the perfection of her face and body. Her features were strong and striking, not easy to forget. With a heart-shaped face, straight nose and plump red lips, she could instantly get a man's blood to pumping with one look, one coquettish expression. Her hair was a mass of sable layers, much shorter than he recalled, and he gripped her tighter against his chest, itching to run his fingers through the cascading tendrils. His mouth watered at the sight of the smooth and milky-tan column of her neck, and he imagined that it would taste as delicious as her cleavage had. His gaze darted to the valley of her breasts displayed within the strange black costume she wore. Already he was harder than he'd ever been before. He could well imagine the feel of her lush and curvaceous body beneath him. All he'd dreamed of since laying eyes on her that first day she'd glided into Perish in 1692, all he'd fantasized about for decades, for centuries, was slaking his lust between her legs.

And exacting his revenge on her.

As he held her warm body against him, he clutched her *trifed* in one hand. He had no idea how he'd known to remove it from her body, nor how he'd known where it was or what its importance was. It had been like an animal instinct. But he wasn't about to let her have it back until he was good and ready — if he ever was ready. Without it, she was powerless.

With it, he was almighty.

He took the outer porch stairs two at a time and kicked open the front door to the inn. Entering the foyer, he scanned it for the stairs. He hadn't been in this particular building since before she'd cursed the town and left him alone, and he now saw that it was worn, dusty and weathered from the hands of time, as were all the structures of Perish. But he well remembered there was a staircase that led to the upper level where it had been rumored that clandestine activities had gone on behind the backs of the upstanding citizens of Perish.

Thanks to the evil siren, he was no longer classified as one of those particular pompous citizens. Not since this woman had instilled a hunger for revenge and lust within his soul. God help him, but he could just strangle her here and now!

Above stairs, it didn't take long to find the suite that would serve his purpose. The door stood ajar, as if to welcome him to his lair of retribution. Crossing the room, he laid her gently upon the canopied bed. The room was lavishly styled in seventeenth-century imported English furnishings. Though Abe had no penchant for such niceties, the room would do perfectly, he thought with anticipation.

But first to secure the *trifed*.

Moving to a nearby dresser, he searched throughout the many drawers until he found a cleverly hidden panel. He placed the triangular witchcraft source within its space then returned to Mia's side.

Kneeling at the raised bedside, he noted a small satchel strapped to her back. Carefully, so as not to awaken her, he removed it from her shoulders. It was made of the same slick black leather her clothing was. Fiddling with the buckles, he drew open the inner flap. *Hmm, rather strange items*, he thought. Reaching in, he removed several devices, all of various sizes, shapes and colors.

He chose one, which closely resembled a man's rod. Holding it up, he turned it from side to side. In so doing, the contraption made a sudden buzzing noise. Abe startled and dropped it next to her slim leg. She moaned, but did not awaken. Quickly, he snatched up the whirring device and his eyes widened in awed response.

The tingly sensation that moved through his fingers, then down into his wrist and forearm was positively mesmerizing. He furrowed his brow as various suspicions coursed through his brain. Cautiously, he touched the faux-cock to his cheek. It sent a rippling pinprick of pleasure down his jaw and throat.

Abe grinned slowly. His gaze swung to the sorceress, lying there all innocent and stripped of her powers. Revenge was going to be so sweet, so very satisfying!

With slow deliberation, he skimmed the contraption down his throat, then over his chest. He sucked in a breath when the tip of the contraption came into contact with one of his nipples. She *was* a witch, he suddenly decided. Only a witch could come up with such a decadent, sinful item as this. Somehow, the thought pleased him, and he felt his cock grow harder with desire for her.

Closing his eyes, he followed his instincts. The buzzing was like sweet music to his ears. Ever so slowly, he drew the tip of the fake penis over his abdomen, then down to the patch of golden hair at the base of his sex. Ripples of desire spread over his skin, but there was no comparison when he joined the strange device parallel with his own hard cock. His large hand went around the two together, and he hissed out in ecstasy as bursts of aching heat shot through him.

"Christ almighty!" he growled and threw his head back, his chest rising and falling in shallow spurts. But he didn't want to lose his ability to exact his revenge on her. With control and patience born and cultivated over the last three centuries, he removed the vibrating item and set it aside. Glancing about the room, he located the perfect tool. Silken drapery ties beckoned to him. He fetched them swiftly and returned to the bed. Within minutes, he had her tied, spread-eagle, across the satin comforter.

God, but she was a beauty! Stepping back, he took his dick in his hand and stroked it as he watched her eyes flutter open.

Red.

Her irises were ruby red, just how he wanted her.
Spitting angry, yet unable to do a thing about it!

Chapter Two

"Afternoon, bright eyes."

The drawl of his voice sent her blood boiling. But not nearly to the level that it reached when she came fully awake to realize that she was tied to the bedposts in a room she'd frequented many times in the distant past.

"You prick." She bucked against her restraints. "Let me go!"

He merely chuckled like a madman.

"Look, Abe. You can't do this to me." She stared at the antique white ceiling, refusing to look at him. "I have more power than you could ever imagine. I can call upon some of the nastiest entities in the universe, and—"

"I have your *trifed* in safe keeping, Mia. Need I say more?"

How did he know about *trifeds*? It was obvious Perish hadn't been equipped with the Internet since she'd been gone. The library was nothing more than a few bookshelves in the foyer of the schoolhouse, which was also his church. The need to learn his source clawed at her insides. Oh, how she hated this man for taking her powers away!

Resentment spewed forth and clouded her judgment. She made the huge mistake of snapping her head to the left to snare him with a hateful stare. That is, until she saw the scrumptious picture he made standing there, feet planted apart, chest puffed out, and one large hand stroking one larger cock. A gush of warmth flooded her G-string. How was it that she could hate him so very thoroughly one second, yet, the next, want him with a yearning that surpassed any she'd ever felt for any man or any wizard in her entire lengthy past?

She sighed with frustration as the afternoon sun shone through the gauzy curtains in misty beams. That's when her gaze caught a glint of light off something metal, something she couldn't quite make out. Stealthily, he moved closer. His thick sex was all but ready to come. She watched, transfixed, as his muscles flexed with his movements.

"Why are you naked?" she asked suddenly. "And why were you already naked when I found you?"

He knelt with one knee upon the bed at the side of her thigh. That was when she realized the metal was a knife he gripped in his non-masturbating hand. Though she did not fear for her life, for Chameleon witches could only die by two day's constant burning, his intent gave her pause.

"I heard you coming," he said huskily. He released his manhood to grip her leather jacket. "I planned ahead, witch. I didn't wish to waste one precious moment with the dispensing of garments..." He inserted the knife between her damp skin and the tough fabric of her jacket. In one swift slice, he had her chest bared. Cool air wafted in through the window, ruffling the curtains and bringing her nipples to life.

"What in the hell do you think you're doing?" she shrieked, yanking against the soft ropes at her wrists and ankles. "Do you know how much that friggin' jacket cost?"

"I told you," he replied smoothly, slicing the knife up first one sleeve, then the other. "I'm not going to waste a minute."

"Don't do the pants. No!" She growled and bucked as he did precisely that.

He stripped the tattered fabric from beneath her, then she looked into eyes the color of insanity. "How can a man of God do this to a woman?" she asked, grasping at anything that might serve as a shield.

He seemed to prowl across the edge of the bed until he hovered on all fours above her. She could smell his spicy scent, his sex, and it brought a renewed flood of fire to her loins. She flicked a look down his sculpted bare chest to the long hard cock that stood poised over her juncture. Spread out as she was, it would probably take one lone stroke inside her, and she'd explode like dynamite.

But she was going to do her damnedest to fight him.

"How can a woman do this to a man of God?" he asked sarcastically. Then he bent his head and pressed his lips softly to hers.

Subtle yet potent tingles of lust pricked her from lips to womb.

"Why is it you can only answer a question with a question?"

He planted his elbows by her shoulders and chuckled. Gently, he held her face in his hands and sucked her bottom lip into his mouth.

"I never was that 'man of God' you always thought I was, Mia."

If it weren't for his mind-blowing admission, she would have succumbed to the excellent mouth-sucking he was currently inflicting on her.

"What?"

He smiled tenderly at her and stared deep into her eyes. She thought that if the world would end now, she would die a most mesmerized witch.

"Technically, I was — until I laid eyes on you."

She stuck out a pouty lip. "Aw. Bad witch entices poor man of God and tempts him to abandon his faith?"

"No," he growled, and his eyes darkened to the black of hatred. "Bad witch casts spell on smitten man and leaves him in solitary confinement for over three centuries. Now man gets his revenge on bad witch."

"And what, aside from restraining me," she asked, tongue-in-cheek as she glanced at her wrists, "can that man do for revenge?"

"Torture," he replied with a honey-thick voice, his eyes gleaming with a mixture of hate and lust. "Sexual torture, my dear Mia, without your precious *trifed* for protection."

"Sorry to disappoint you, dear Abraham, but sex is not torture to me. I delight in it, live for it, crave its very existence in my long, immortal life."

"Really? Well, we shall see..." He captured her lips then in a quite torturous kiss. The blade of his tongue swept her mouth with a hunger that fed her own. She longed to wrap her arms around him, but the ropes impeded her desire. And yet, somehow, the very thought of being denied that which she yearned, was an aphrodisiac in and of itself. The coals smoldered and smoked. Tiny flames leaped toward prized kindling as his mouth left hers to trail kisses down her neck, to her heaving breasts. Shivers engulfed her, and he claimed one pearl just as it tightened in response to his oncoming assault. One lone burst of heat exploded and spread over her flesh, invading the tender nerves of her pussy.

His hands were all over her, and she rejoiced that her legs were already spread for him. He swirled his tongue in her navel, and a tug of warmth oozed through her system. Instinctively, she lifted her pelvis, gyrating against his chest as he moved lower still. His tongue did a delicious dance, and forged a trail from her lower abdomen, around her sensitive sex, to her inner thighs. With adept male skill, he snatched up the knife and sliced away the g-string, baring her completely to his hot gaze. He parted her folds with the fingers of one hand, and she sucked in a breath as he slid one, then two fingers into her damp cavern.

"You're already wet, love," he said huskily, his breath now coming in warm puffs across her clit. "But not nearly as wet as you're going to get…"

She desperately needed her legs free so that she could clamp them around his neck and hold his face against her cunt. "Please…Abe…untie me."

She heard him moan and inhale her scent. Then his tongue sliced wickedly upward from the lower edge of her vulva to the patch of hair over her pubic bone. He was deliberately avoiding the one spot she needed him to attend to most.

Then she heard one of her vibrators come to life.

* * * * *

Abe held up the next contraption in her bag of tricks and inspected it as the rays of the late afternoon sun streamed in and cast a golden glow upon its skin-toned surface. It was silky-soft and U-shaped with bumpy knots running up and down the length of it, one leg's bulges twice as large as the other. He moved his finger over a square protrusion at the outer curve and gasped when it slid a mere fraction of an inch. In response, the apparatus glowed bright pink and vibrated against his palm.

Instinct flooded his mind and his eyes flicked to her vee. It dribbled with rich cream. The pearly juice ran a trail from her feminine sex to her anus, tight and unyielding. He licked his lips and struggled to ignore the thickening ache in his groin. Despite being stripped of her witch's *trifed*, she continued to entice him with her charms. Spread wide for him, there was nothing left for him to do but fill her holes with the quivering tool.

Her eyes flared and changed from red to black. "Don't you touch me!" she warned, struggling against the ropes. "*That* one I need to control myself!"

His response was to lower the buzzing instrument between her legs. Then, maddeningly, he dragged the U-shaped toy up one inner thigh.

From the deep black of her hate, her eyes swirled and glowed, shifting to a glowing blue. Passion. The blue had always indicated passion and strong emotion.

"Please…" she begged. Her breathing became shallow, and she stilled her frantic movements. Her tongue came out, wet and satiny against her lips, as he slowly drew the tip of one end up into the tender flesh where her leg joined with her pussy. Her vulva lips were swollen now, and he had but to inhale minutely to catch the sweet essence of her arousal.

He growled when she sucked in a sharp breath at his next careful placement of the device — the large-knotted leg at the opening of her female channel and the small-knotted leg pressed against her tight asshole.

And he shoved the wondrous gadget deep into her cores.

"By the powers of the Chameleons," she breathed it out, her head thrashing, her eyes flickering between sapphire, ruby and onyx, "I will curse you into eternity if you do not end this madness!"

He chuckled as she twitched and moaned. But his revenge was not to be that simple. Though his eyes took in the luscious curve of her breasts, the nipples tight with passion, he wanted to first get right to the crux of things.

Abe then lowered his head and swiped her clit with his tongue. As he pushed and pulled the curved device in and out of her, he drove her mad with his tongue, up and down, all around, back and forth. She tasted of sweet buttery cream, and he gorged on the unique, addictive flavor of her.

She screamed as if the fires of a witch's flame were engulfing her with sweet death. "Abe…" she whimpered. "I'm going to come right—"

In tune to her body and the harmony of her husky voice, he abruptly lifted his head and yanked the device from her inner channels.

She gasped, her body going from rigid to limp. "No!" she snarled. "You bastard!" Her eyes, now glowing blood-red orbs, sliced down the naked length of her own body to snare him with her ire.

He looked up at her from his place between her legs. "My sweet revenge has only just begun," he warned. Then a different sort of animalistic urge swept him. His gaze fell upon her plump parted lips as she drew air in and out of her lungs. A tenderness followed, and he realized he suddenly longed to cover her angry mouth with his own.

Chapter Three

Mia was enraged. And on fire.

Did he really think he could get away with this?

A wild fear choked her very soul. Yes. As long as he had her tied up, and her *trifed* hidden, she was doomed to be at his mercy.

And, mercy, but he had the talent of a warlock's touch! Who would have ever thought a man of the clergy could put such a torturous hex on a woman, and least of all, Mia Foxe, High Priestess of the Chameleon Coven?

So, she thought as he stealthily crawled up her body on all fours, he was going to get his long-awaited revenge by torturing her, by bringing her to the brink of ecstasy time and time again.

He was going to drive her sexually mad, and deny her the ultimate release of orgasm!

The thought of it both thrilled and frustrated her. If only she could get loose…

"It's no use, my poor little captured witch," he purred. His face was but a breath from hers. The tip of his dick brushed her pussy, zapping her with desire. She closed her eyes and willed the ultimate to happen. Gorgon, but she wished he would just shove his cock right into her wetness!

He lowered his head and softly touched his lips to hers. A glow of warmth spread through her veins and ignited each and every cell in her body.

"Why do you carry around that bag of contraptions?" he suddenly asked.

She opened her eyes to look deep into the depths of his soul. His long flaxen hair shone in stark contrast to the darkness of his eyes, now soft with an indefinable emotion. They twinkled, and she thought of a night sky during the summer solstice, vast and infinite.

She shrugged as best as she could within the confines of the restraints. "A Chameleon needs sexual release at least once daily. It is like a mortal man's need for oxygen and food. It 'recharges' the soul."

He nodded, as if he fully understood the nature of a Chameleon. "But why use the devices, and not a man?" His voice was low, soft, and he dragged his lips back and forth across hers as he spoke.

Mia inhaled, her eyelids fluttered, she felt her engine revive and shift into a new gear of desire. "I said," she replied, her lips chasing his in an effort to plunge her tongue into his sweet mouth, "*at least* once daily. Me? I require more than any man can give me."

"Ah…so you're insatiable," he breathed, his penis probing entry into her dampness. "And you cannot find a man to give you all you require. So you pleasure yourself in between."

"Precisely." Raising her head, she captured his lips before he could evade her. His tongue sliced through her mouth with the sharpness of a blade. A renewed flood of moisture oozed from between her legs and her system quickened. One of his hands slid up her rib cage and cupped her breast. She moaned into his mouth as he pinched the nipple between his thumb and forefinger, then pulled on it until it snapped free of his hold. Shards of glass seemed to cut through to her spirit. At that very instant, he pushed his long shaft into her. Yet he held back, denying her its full length.

"You are an evil sorcerer," she accused, panting. He ignored her and began a trek down her neck, nipping, kissing, licking. She struggled to suppress the trembling of her limbs, the instinctual rise of her hips.

I will hide my desire from you. I will have my precious orgasms…and you will be none the wiser!

At the exact moment the thought had formed in her mind, his mouth closed over one nipple. He tweaked the other simultaneously. An inferno swept through her, and she bucked against her restraints, desperate for his cock to fully penetrate her. She heard her own groan and quickly bit her lip to stifle the automatic response. She would be damned if she'd cue him to the fact that release was but inches, mere seconds away…

He rocked against her, but refused to completely impale himself in her.

Then, as if he'd dumped an entire cauldron of cold water on her, he yanked his cock from inside her and leapt to tower over her at the bedside. His sex was long and beautiful, and, if she weren't bound to the bedposts, it would be within blessed reach of her greedy hands. She itched to take its silk-coated steel into her mouth, deep into her throat, to taste the pre-cum that now, at this very moment, dribbled from the slit. His manhood glistened from tip to halfway down its length, her own pearly juices wrapped lusciously around its thickness.

"What now?" she asked, gazing up into the glazed chocolate of his eyes.

"You'll see, my enchantress," he said cryptically as he backed away from the bedside. "You'll see…"

* * * * *

He reached for the canvas that had been folded neatly atop the dresser where he'd tucked her *trifed*. Kneeling at her side, he lifted her hips and stuffed the rough cloth beneath her, straightening it so that it was a neat square beneath her sprawled body. On each of four corners, there was an embedded brass ring. He leaned toward the bedside table that held several interesting items, and chose two thick ropes. Twining each through opposite corners and crisscrossing them over her, he then took the free ends and inserted them into the metal loop that hung from the canopy frame.

"What do you think you're doing?"

He risked a look at her, and his heart nearly fell from his chest. Her eyes were now green, a sign she was somehow finding humor in the situation. Her skin was aglow with passion, glistening with a fine sheen of perspiration. The thick mass of her hair was fanned around her face like a halo of rich mink. With her lips bruised, swollen and moist from his kisses, and her full breasts thrust upward, she was a pure vision of loveliness. Her slim waist flared to hips that were rounded to exaggeration by her widely spread legs. And the neatly trimmed thatch of dark hair at the crown of her sex called up wicked spirits he'd never before encountered in his pre-spell days of mortal existence.

She exuded danger, decadence, pure black magic.

She had already bewitched him from the moment he'd heard the rumble of her strange mode of transportation barreling through the spell's field into his lonely world. Nay, from the moment he'd laid eyes on her in 1692.

"Imposing my revenge on you, sweet, sweet, Mia," he finally replied. He did not try to hide the resentment in his voice. "Have you already forgotten that you cast a spell on me hundreds of years ago, and left me to rot in my own solitary loneliness? Can you not fathom what torture it is not to see another mortal human being for so very long, not to touch one, converse with one? Not to make love to one, for heaven's sake? You, who requires more than one release daily, cannot see this?" Abe was now trembling with anger. But he was in control, for there was no other way for him but this. He released one of her wrists so that she could rise halfway. She automatically lifted her torso, propped now on her free elbow. He tugged on both ropes until the corners rose around her. Then, when he was certain she was cocooned safely, so as not to allow escape, he released the remaining wrist. "Sit up within the canvas," he ordered.

She rubbed her wrists and glared at him, though her eyes remained green. Nonetheless, she sat up fully until the fabric was just below chin level. "Sit up? With my legs strung painfully wide and this scratchy fabric between my damn legs?"

He pulled again on the cord until the slack lessoned and she became enslaved within the fabric nest. Then he released her ankles. "Now, draw your feet in so that your knees are pressed against your breasts."

She sighed and tested the limberness of her legs. After a brief caress of her ankles, she obeyed. Assured that her bottom was centered over the hole in the canvas, he hauled her up in one smooth move until her body was suspended approximately one foot from the surface of the mattress.

"Abe…" He watched as her eyes turned a strange shade of yellow. "Abe, I'm scared. Please let me down from here." Fear. Yellow must equal fear. It was the very first time he'd ever seen her eyes turn the color of butter.

He secured the rope and climbed onto the bed. Lying down on his back, he positioned himself under her suspended form. He could see her pussy through the hole in the canvas, and he wiggled and scooted until it was directly over his erection. Anticipation throbbed in his groin, threatening premature release. Her wicked female scent taunted him, enflamed his senses with unbridled sexual need. He could see the moist slit tighten with her anxiety, and he longed to soothe its stickiness, to lap up the balm of her desire and give her what she craved.

But he wouldn't…yet.

"Relax, Mia." Within the three-inch strategically placed round hole, his finger found her folds and parted them. He heard her suck in a sharp breath, then whimper with longing. "I'm not going to hurt you."

"Please," she said, her body sagging downward when he slowly inserted one finger inside her canal. "Don't torture me this way anymore. I…I promise… If you give me back my *trifed*, I will reverse the—oh!"

His hands had moved to her hips, and he now had himself buried completely inside her. He closed his eyes and struggled to tamp down the rising orgasm. It had been well over three hundred years since his cock had been gloved to the hilt by something other than his own hand.

Willing his mind to think of anything but her tight wetness, he gripped her ass and twisted her canvassed bulk like a corkscrew upon his dick.

Chapter Four

Mia groaned as the new sensation assaulted her. Never before had she been fucked in corkscrew fashion. As he slowly twisted her cocoon over his cock, fragments of random yearnings stabbed into her. By the alternating angles of his tool, coupled with the tilt of her own passage, the circular motion within her womb was mind-boggling. With each rotation, she was gradually being lifted until only the head of his shaft was inside her. She looked up and saw that the ropes were now twisted to their absolute maximum tautness. For one split second, she could hear them scrape against the metal ring formed inside the canopy frame.

"Are you ready, love?" she heard him say hoarsely, his voice coated with restrained lust.

"Yes!" she couldn't help but shout. "Yes, I'm ready!"

And he let go.

There was a brief pause where all was still.

Then round and round she went.

"Holy Hazel!" she screeched. Her head was spinning pleasantly. There was the whir of the contraption as it unraveled, along with the scent of her stirred juices wafting through the air. Following her own initial reaction, she could hear his muttered groans. With each rotation, her tightness plunged further and further down upon his cock, encasing him tightly within her cunt. She was so close to release, she could almost taste its luscious flavor in her mouth. It reached for her with tantalizing wings of sin.

Then the ride ceased. Completely unraveled, the rope twisted the opposite direction by half a turn then it straightened until she was halted motionless on top of him.

The orgasm, so near she'd felt its first wave, was now gone.

"Oh!" she said with a clenched jaw. "You are maddening, evil, a man of the cruelest nature!"

He spoke not a word and repeated the torture over and over again, twisting her bulk then releasing it. Each time, she cried out for the blessed orgasm to take her. Each time, it was denied her.

He swung her at an angle and she felt his abrupt withdrawal. A cold loneliness seeped into her soul.

"And casting a three-century-long spell on me wasn't cruel?" he barked.

She ignored his obvious point. "Let me out of here," she ordered, wriggling and squirming so that she could stand up in the canvas.

He rose from the bed and snatched up a sheet. He wrapped it around his waist then strode to the door. Plucking up the skeleton key, he closed the door completely and inserted the key in the keyhole. He turned it until there was a resounding *click*.

She scrambled from the confines of her prison and watched warily as he crossed to the window and tossed the key out into the oncoming light of dusk. She heard its *cling-clang* as it hit several items on the way down.

"I can climb out the window," she warned, clambering from the confines of the suspended canvas.

He slanted her a look of pure amusement. "Not when I'm in the room, you can't."

She rolled her eyes and then studied his lithe movements. He was like a panther on the hunt as he located her backpack again. She watched, entranced, as his manhood remained erect while he rummaged through the bag's contents. His cock almost seemed to be about to burst, it was so very thick and engorged. Her heartbeat thrummed against her lungs, impeding her breathing. He was a beautiful specimen, she admitted. Why hadn't she seen it long ago? Shit, why hadn't she just cast a spell on him back then so she could've had her way with him?

Answers evaded her. She shrugged the questions off. More importantly at hand was how to remedy the torment he seemed to be delighting in bestowing upon her.

But her mind continued to whirl with self-doubt and confusion.

Why had she been compelled to seek him out? Why today of all days in the last centuries?

She didn't know the answers to any of her questions. All she knew was that he was obviously imprisoning her for one thing, and one thing only. Revenge.

He pilfered through the backpack for several more minutes, examining each item in turn, then finally appeared satisfied with a particular find.

"What now, tease?" she asked, collapsing on the bed. He was never going to relieve her of her sexual frustrations, she decided gloomily. And suddenly, a thought occurred to her. Was she destined to spend eternity here with him, forbidden to experience full release as punishment for her Chameleon's spell upon him?

The thought frightened her beyond measure. Without her *trifed*, and never being allowed to fuel her Chameleon witch's soul, she would surely shrivel up and literally die, despite her supposed immortality. With the exception of the early years after her birth, she had never gone one day in her life without an orgasm. As a result, she had emerged a strong and victorious witch, and had rightly earned her title of High Priestess of the Chameleon Coven.

What now?

Would she be stripped of the title? Would she truly die? Or would she be damned to this tempting man's wrath forever?

Gorgon, help her if that is the case!

* * * * *

"Candy coated chocolates," he read carefully. The dark brown bag with white letters was odd but interesting. He glanced up at her where she remained sprawled naked on the bed. "What's this?"

Her melodious chuckle reached his ears wrapped in a smooth layer of sex. "It's candy. And they're my favorite."

"Candy. Hmmm. May I?"

The emerald of her eyes glistened from across the room. "Be my guest," she replied blandly.

As he tore open the bag, he watched her draw up her legs and plunge one hand down over her curves until it reached her pussy. "Take your hand from there—now," he replied calmly.

She sighed, disgusted, and removed the strumming fingers from her swollen clit. Then she rolled over onto her stomach and punched the bed. "You're going to regret this."

Yes, he was already regretting the fact that his alter-ego insisted on carrying through with his much needed vengeance. He wondered if his reprisals were hurting himself more than Mia. The luscious curve of her ass called to him, and from his place across the room he had a perfect view of her slick sex-lips. Oh, how he longed to sate his lust between her legs.

And he would eventually, he assured himself. Patience. *Patience and you will have it all*, he thought.

He shook the bag and peered inside. There were hundreds of round items in various bright colors. He slid a finger in and drew out a blue one. Blue like her eyes when he was buried inside her. He sniffed it, then slowly inserted it into his mouth. He rolled it around on his tongue before biting into it. A dark yet sweet flavor burst in his mouth.

"Delicious!" he mumbled.

She suddenly rolled over and sat upright. "May I have some?"

He stared at her for a long moment. "Soon."

Then she plopped back onto the bed and spat, "Fuck!"

Fuck, indeed, he thought. He set aside the candy and reached into the leather sack again. His fingers closed over a square little slick object. He held it up, and perused it carefully.

Lubricated Latex Condom, it read.

He could smell the faint, yet sharp odor of…what, he wasn't sure. Then he tore open the pale blue package and studied the disc-shaped item. It was soft and somewhat slick in his fingers, and the aroma of the article intensified as he removed it from its casing. "And this? What, may I ask, is it?"

She flicked a bored gaze his way then a positively evil grin crossed her lovely face. "It's a condom. It slides over a man's—um, cock, er—um, sex organ. It prevents pregnancy and shields against disease."

Fascinating! "Really?"

"Really. Wanna try it on me?" she said slyly.

Yes, he wanted to try it on her. He tossed aside the wrapper and stuck one finger into the center, and slowly unrolled the condom so that it gloved his forefinger. His eyes shifted to the bag of candy. Without a moment's hesitation, he removed the condom from his finger, turned it upside-down, then he slid a dozen or so candies into its opening.

"What in the hell are you doing?" she asked, obviously appalled. "It's not a candy sack."

"Thinking of yet another way to settle the score."

"With *those*?" Her voice was disbelieving and somewhat ridiculing.

But he'd show her. Pinching the opening shut until it was against the head of his penis, he released it and slid and tugged until the condom, lumpy with the round candies, completely encasing him. Strategically, he moved the candies under the surface this way and that so that his manhood resembled a club with many colorful warts upon its surface. He throbbed within the condom as the smooth surface of the candies held tightly against him, played havoc on his senses and further increased his arousal. Now, all he could think of was plunging himself inside her, and discovering what new sensations his unique idea would give them.

"You're kidding me, right?" she asked. But she didn't wait for his response. Her throaty giggle filled the room, further inflaming him.

Without replying, he sauntered over to the bed and looked down at her. And he would never, in all of eternity, forget the sudden drugged, passionate expression of expectation upon her gorgeous face as her laughter died and she looked up at his candied cock.

Chapter Five

Wow! Two of her favorites all wrapped up in one scrumptious package!

Her heart suddenly ceased beating. As her mouth watered and she yearned to take his sweet cock between her lips, her eyes rose to meet his. There was something there, something altogether new and mesmerizing.

Free now to touch him, she reached up and closed her hand over the condom, never taking her eyes from his. They were chocolate, like the insides of her favourite . He hissed in a breath, but did not speak. Her pussy began to throb as if it had a heartbeat of its own. A cold-hot sensation flooded her witch's system.

"I want you," he said, his voice thick and deep.

"Make love to me," she whispered.

Just then, the last rays of sunlight faded from the room. Dusk blew in through the open shutters on a cool night breeze. There was the scent of smoke from a far-off chimney mingled with the new harvest. Her eyes adjusted to the dimness, and she watched as his form moved nearer. Releasing him, she allowed him to kneel between her legs, and she held her arms up in welcome as he slowly covered her body with his. A strange and comforting warmth eased into her muscles, into her very heart.

It was the first time she'd been allowed to explore him. Her hands glided over his sinewy back, explored every smooth angle and plane. His manhood probed her gently while his chest abraded her nipples, turning them into aching buds of fire. Then his mouth touched hers whisper-soft.

"Mia..." he said huskily.

"Abe...I...I..." She panted it out. It was all she could do not to beg and scream. Kneading his spine, her hands traveled lower toward his buttocks—until he reached behind himself and stilled her movements.

"Keep your hands above my waist."

"But...but why?" The sudden stern tone to his voice had struck a tender chord within her. She wanted to explore every inch of him, every cell.

His only answer was to plunge himself inside her.

"Oh! Holy, Medusa!" The candy within the condom had further thickened him, true, but it was the random knots grinding over every nerve ending within her pussy as he throbbed in restraint, that drove her to madness.

"Mia..." he said again, and she knew then that he would not be able to continue to curb his lust, to deny her.

It was the perfect opportunity to get one of her daily orgasms in...*finally*! She didn't waste time. Her legs flew up and clamped tightly at his back. She shoved her arms under his and curled her hands up and over his beefy shoulders. Gripping him for leverage, she lifted her ass and slammed herself up against him.

There was no escape for him now, she thought, pleased and full of a desperate need. He was hers for as long as she wanted him!

He groaned in response, then slid his hands beneath her buttocks and gathered her close. She had never been so thoroughly filled in her entire existence! Nerve endings she had no idea existed, were stimulated by the candied length of him. He rocked his hips, then, and drove himself into her time and time again. Ecstasy beckoned to her. She could feel its outer edges moving in toward her womb in white-hot waves.

He pumped her ruthlessly, calling out her name over and over again. She slid her damp channel instinctively over the condom as multicolored rays of desire shattered around them. Mia had never before seen such a magical display with the act of sex. It seemed to further enhance her orgasm, lengthening and intensifying it to mind-boggling proportions.

Together, they cried out as a beautiful glow filled the room.

* * * * *

He looked down into her Chameleon eyes at that very moment of release. They were swirled with every color of the rainbow. She convulsed beneath him, her soft, damp skin gliding over his. The song of her release filled his heart. In every way, physically, mentally, emotionally, he felt the culmination of his destiny at that orgasmic instant.

The first step, the morphing, was now complete. Further knowledge and understanding poured into him.

But she didn't have to know that at the moment. All he could think to do was claim her. He was on the path to making her his woman. The thought filled him with both joy and sadness.

Sadness, for he was aware she would never give up her independence for an eternity with him.

She purred then, like a sated cat. Stirring, she scratched her witch's claws across his shoulders. "That was totally earth-shattering!"

"Yes," he agreed, easing himself from her slickness. "Your favorite candy has suddenly become mine."

She giggled like an innocent schoolgirl. "I want to eat them," she insisted, pressing him up and away from her. He came up on his knees in the bed and watched as she sat up. Her hand closed over the base of his shaft. *Son of a bitch, but I will never get enough of her!* he thought as desire flared anew in him.

"Eat them?"

"Yes." To prove her point, she pinched the tip of the condom where his jism filled the small space, and slowly unrolled it from his cock. From the heat of her passage, coupled with his own sexual fire, she revealed the candy that had melted in splatters over his thickness. The morsels still clung sweetly to him in colorful random splotches. Tossing aside the used latex, she licked her plump lips as her eyes glowed aqua, a mixture of humor and passion. When awareness at what she intended to do, dawned on him, he groaned on a long sigh.

Grasping the base of his rising sex, she snaked out her tongue and slurped one spot of chocolate from him, the red cracked candy pieces prickling into his rod. Next, she chose one off to the side, green smeared with brown. Pursing her lips over it, she suckled it from him, licking his skin to a state of clean and clear hardness.

His balls drew up in anticipation. Pre-cum oozed from his slit. He reached out his hands and cupped both of her mounds, pinching and pulling the nipples until she whimpered her satisfaction. Despite the distraction, she continued her journey. Up next came a brown candy, then a bright orange one. Set upon the front side of the head was one the color of her fear. Yellow. Without so much as a moment of hesitation, she closed her mouth over the tip and swirled her tongue around the sensitive head.

"Oh, Mia!" he growled. "If you don't stop, I'll —"

She had no intention of stopping. When she'd swallowed the last remnants of the sweet morsels, she opened wide and closed her mouth over him, gloving him with the depths of her throat. A volcano deep within his soul boiled and threatened to spew. Bobbing her head, she gripped the base of him with one hand, and his sac with the other. Mercilessly, she sucked him off, his body going taut with lust. Interwoven with it was a strange element of tenderness and intimacy for this witch who had driven him to the bowels of insanity with her curse.

Now she'd cast a different spell upon him. Though it was much more bearable, it was just as intense, just as damning in its own way.

And he didn't want it any other way.

The lava was building. Its orange glow coursed throughout his system, scalding him wherever it touched. A slow crescendo of chaotic rumbling formed, and he combed his hands through her hair, clutching her skull so that he could move her head in the perfect rhythm. He heard her muffled moan of satisfaction, and her tongue twirled eagerly around him. Then nature took its course. He trembled with the volcano, and the power of it built to unbearable strengths. There was no turning back. The boiling fire of his lust spewed forth, and he heard her swallow in greedy gulps.

It was then that he collapsed, resigned to the fact that he'd never be fully satisfied with revenge. Exhausted, he dragged her down with him and curled behind her, tucking her against his heart.

Finally, for the first time in over three long centuries, he slept like a contented baby.

Chapter Six

Mia awoke to the sound of chirping birds. Dawn was barely casting its light into the room. They were twined together in a pocket of warmth, the blankets tangled about them haphazardly. She could swear she smelled apples and spice upon the chilly morning breeze as it swished into the room. She was hungry, she admitted silently, her stomach rumbling in agreement. But a witch did not require a mortal's food. It was merely an indulgence, unlike sex and the requirement of orgasms.

She closed her eyes again and basked in the sensation of warmth and contentment his nearness caused within her heart.

But she didn't need it. She needed her *trifed.*

Gently, she lifted his arm from her waist and slid from the curve of his body. Harsh, cold air assaulted her. She shivered, but ignored the discomfort. Setting his arm down upon the mattress, she studied his face in slumber. His lashes curved in dark fans over his cheeks. The chiseled, handsome sculpture of his face, along with the contented curve of his mouth, made her long to cup his jaw and kiss him tenderly. The long strands of sandy hair were brushed away from his face, and she could see beautiful flecks of gold shining here and there as the sun's dim morning rays filtered into the room. She reached out a hand to brush one lock from his cheek.

Then she ceased her movement and curled her hand into a fist.

No. She must locate her witch's source immediately, and flee before he awakened. Stealthily, she crept from their bed of fire. She first searched the closet, next the hope chest at the foot of the bed, then the side table. Clamping her lower lip between her teeth, she worried over the possibility that she would never find it. Then she moved to the mahogany dresser. It contained a dozen or so drawers. With patience and adeptness, she searched each drawer, moving aside silky nightdresses and lacy garters.

Just when she was about to give up and move her search to another side of the room, her hand brushed a tiny protuberance at the back of a lower drawer. Heart thumping, she pulled on the knob.

Her *trifed*! She'd found it!

Gripping its skin-textured triangle shape, she closed her eyes and rejoiced in the energy that zapped through her at first contact. It glowed pink, as if to say that it had missed her. She threw a look across the room at him.

Now you're powerless against me, Abraham Warwick. Your vengeance is finally at its end.

And so was her spell.

She quickly reached behind her and found the indentation at her spine's base. Aligning it perfectly, she clicked it into its rightful place.

Spears of jagged lightening sliced through the ceiling and encompassed her. She raised her arms in acceptance, and closed her eyes as the orgasm slammed into her. Inhaling deeply, Mia rejoiced in her revival.

She was whole again.

Chanting, she now called upon the coven entities. Her mind scanned its embedded files of spells. Locating the correct one, she hummed and sang, reversing the curse she'd damned him to that day long ago in 1692 when he'd threatened to burn her alive. He'd never find her now. She would be safe from his wrath.

His beautiful body would resume its mortal state of aging and existence. He'd be allowed to leave the boundaries of Perish. He might encounter a bit of culture shock, but he'd survive. In addition, the spell field surrounding Perish would now dissolve. People would return. Perish would be rebuilt and begin to thrive, though in a much more modern fashion. And its legend of a Chameleon's spell would be the very thing that would draw tourists to satisfy their curiosity of the haunted grounds and its notable history.

Moving on to the next task at hand, she flicked a hand and conjured up a silent chant. Obediently, her leather garments rose and embraced her. The tattered edges sealed upward in zipper fashion.

She was ready to fly.

Taking one last longing look at him, she leaped into the air and morphed into a white dove, her wings flapping softly as she hovered over his body. But she didn't dally long. Taking flight, she glided through the open window and spotted her motorbike.

It was time to get the hell out of Dodge.

* * * * *

The roaring noise awoke him. Abe sat upright in bed. "Huh?" Confusion clouded his mind at first then he was struck by raw consciousness. The room was cold, but all he could feel was the vibrations of the motor as it was revved below in the town courtyard.

"Mia?" He glanced about the room. His eyes snapped with awareness. Gradually, his gaze lowered to the empty spot in the bed next to him. His hand shot out and he fisted the warmth of the sheets where she had laid with him all through the night. Already, he was hard for her, his cock jutting upward thick and tight. But she was gone.

Scrambling from bed, he shot across the room. Planting his hands on the windowsill, he leaned out and caught a glimpse of her leather-clad form just before she took off like a bat out of hell and disappeared into the copse of trees.

Driven by a frantic mood of his own, he whirled and went straight to the dresser. Amid various others, the drawer where he'd hidden her *trifed* was standing ajar. Garments from their innards were strewn haphazardly about. So, he thought grimly, she'd found her precious life force. She was back to being the almighty, invincible witch.

He shoved a hand through his long tresses. Would she have reversed the spell? Was he again damned to solitary confinement?

"Well, Abe," he said solemnly. "There's only one way to find out."

He'd locked himself in, he suddenly remembered, but it was of no importance. Naked, he climbed out the window onto the inn's porch overhang. Scooting cautiously downward, he scaled the edge, turned onto his stomach and dropped to the dirt ground below.

With haste born of centuries of pent-up emotions, he strode through the desolate village to his home at the far edge. Ducking, he entered the low portal, the door still standing ajar from his excited flight of less than twenty-four hours ago. His clothing remained on the stone floor near the hearth where he'd quickly stripped when he'd heard — no, sensed — her arrival yesterday afternoon.

Quickly, angrily, he bent and retrieved the garments, then shoved his limbs into them methodically, one by one. On his way out the door, he plucked his cape and hat from a peg upon the wall.

Stepping out into the cool morning air, the sun just then peeping through the forest trees, he tipped his head back and shut his eyes. Inhaling, he drew in her unique scent as it fluttered along with the autumn breeze.

Now to test the boundaries of the spell.

He was ready.

But was she?

Chapter Seven

"Next time," Sue Morrow said with a scolding, motherly tone, "you let me know you're going to be gone all night long. I almost called the police," she added, turning from the window. She was watching for her fiancé to arrive. They had purchased a home not far from Mia's old Victorian on the outskirts of Salem. Today was the closing on the loan at the bank. Mia had been thrilled for her roommate and best friend. James and Sue were perfect for one another. But now the cruel clutches of envy gripped her. She'd never before felt that particular rancid emotion.

Until today.

"Sorry," Mia mumbled. "I had a very important matter to attend to."

Sue turned back to the window and parted the drapes. "That I was aware of by the way you suddenly leapt from your spot in front of the TV and flew out the door. Just give me a heads up from now on. You could have called on your cell phone after leaving, ya know? I worry —"

Her abrupt halt of words sent a sudden swirl of dread through Mia's stomach. Mia had a clear view of Sue's profile. Her jaw was now practically resting on her chest. Her soft gray eyes slowly widened as she stared out the window.

"Sue, honey, what's wrong?"

"Holy hell," she croaked.

"Believe me, hell is not holy," Mia said, hoping to lighten the mood in the room. Her friend had no idea she was an immortal witch, but Mia had always delighted in dropping subtle nuances of herself to Sue. Sue had never caught on.

Before Sue could reply, the foyer door flew open and crashed against the floral wallpaper Mia had just hung days ago. Like a woman with a nesting instinct toward the end of a pregnancy, Mia had oddly been cleaning and remodeling her drafty old home for the last several months.

"Mia Foxe!"

From her place in the parlor, she didn't have a view of the front door, but there was no mistaking that voice.

It was Abraham. Dread turned to fear. She averted her gaze, for she knew her eyes were yellow now, and she wasn't prepared to scare the shit out of her friend at the moment.

She shot to her feet from the recliner where she'd been crocheting. The yarn and hook fell to the floor. "Abe!" she whispered.

"Abe?" Sue asked, clearly confused. Just then, a horn tooted at the street side curb. "Mia, what's going on?"

Abe strode in at that moment. Mia's gaze was drawn helplessly to him, and her heart fluttered at the regal sight of him clad in an off-white linen shirt with a close-fitting earthy green doublet. She noted that he was attired in the fashionable laced collar and cuffs of the point in history for which she'd banished him. Her eyes shifted lower to the knee-length breeches, opaque stockings and low-heeled black leather shoes. They were just as he'd worn them back then, and a nostalgic thrill went through her veins.

Upon his head he sported a felt hat, and it was tipped at a most rakish angle, his long hair gathered into a ribbon at his back. A dark cloak clung to his broad shoulders and fanned about him like a vampire. He was dashingly handsome—he simply took her breath away!

But his eyes were black with rage. He flicked his gaze here, then there, until he found her. And her heart plummeted to her feet.

"Don't worry…" Mia said to Sue, never taking her eyes from Abe. She willed her mood to change to one of humor so that her eyes were green for Sue's benefit. The tingling behind her eyes told her the transformation was a success. With it, her heart rate slowed. "It's fine. You run along now. I hear James honking for you."

"But—"

"Go!"

Sue slid her gaze up and down Abe. "Mister," she said, her upper lip curled like a protective mother bear, "if you lay one hand on her, I swear I'll tear you limb from limb." She took several hesitant steps across the room toward the door, toward Abe where he filled the arched parlor doorway.

Abe's gaze finally left Mia. He soaked Sue with an assessing stare. "Miss, you can just bet that I'm the one in danger here, not the witch."

Sue folded her arms at the derogatory remark. She bounced her eyes from man to woman. Outdoors, James tooted his horn impatiently. "Mia, I don't have to go. We can change the closing date to another day."

"No." Shaking the shock from her brain, Mia finally lifted her feet where they'd been glued to the hardwood floor, and crossed the room to stand before Abe. Already, she could smell his spicy scent, and her blood thrummed like a she-wolf in heat. "I'll be fine, Sue. It's just an old friend…"

Abe merely snorted at that.

Sue's eyes narrowed. "Are you *sure*?"

"Yes," Mia said without taking her eyes from Abe's handsome face. "I'm very sure."

There was a long pause in which Sue studied them, wavering with her decision.

"Oh, well…in that case, I guess I'll skeddadle along," she replied hesitantly. After another indecisive delay, she added, "You're sure, now?"

Mia nodded. "Bye, Sue. I'll be here when you return to help you move your things into the new house."

That reminder elicited a sunny expression from Sue. "Yes, the move. Well, I'll leave you to your…friend." She stepped around Abe's bulk and swept him with one last look. As she entered the foyer, Mia heard her mumble, "Very, very hot man, but strange costume."

The click of the door closing echoed in the entryway. The grandfather clock in the parlor corner ticked and tocked. They stared at one another for a long moment.

"You thought I wouldn't find you, didn't you, Mia?" His voice, slightly accented, was accusatory. He stepped into the room so that they were toe to toe.

Mia's gaze rose slowly. She stared boldly into his dark eyes. "How did you find me?"

"You lifted the spell, obviously."

"I know that," she said with irritation. "How did you *find* me?"

He shrugged. "Instinct." That was when his irises swirled like a marble from black to green.

She gasped and backed away. "What the...?"

He took two steps toward her and closed the gap. "What's the matter, Mia? You look as if you've seen a...witch."

With that, he grinned, though his eyes twinkled with an evil shade of emerald. He removed his hat and tossed it across the floor. Next came his cape. Swiping it from his broad shoulders, he flung it onto the nearby divan. As she backed away, he neared. With each step he took, another hook, another button, was released. Off came his shirt and shoes. Mia's gaze sank to his crotch. Already, his manhood strained to be released from his breeches. As if in answer to her inner yearnings, he stepped out of the pants and stockings, and stood naked before her.

She couldn't take her eyes from his sex. A hunger coursed through her womb. She dragged in a ragged breath and knew the precise moment her eyes morphed to the blue of passion. Slowly, her gaze rose to his.

And they were blue also.

"I don't understand!" she gasped. "How can this be?"

He turned, almost deliberately, and purposely placed his trousers on the chair where, only minutes ago, she'd been contentedly crocheting. Her heart ceased beating. At the base of his spine, just above the crack of his ass, was a *trifed*!

"No!" she gasped.

He turned back and his smile was gone. Though his cock remained erect, his eyes had turned back to black. With his hands in tight fists, he took slow deliberate steps toward her. She flung up a hand and the antique lamp on an end table crashed on the floor at his feet. He looked down at it, then up at her. He stepped calmly over it.

"Stay away from me!" she warned. His eyes were narrowed now with anger. She hummed and upturned the divan. One corner crashed onto his foot, but he didn't flinch. "What do you think you're doing?" she screeched, fear now clutching at her gut, for she accepted the fact that she was up against a warlock that had every right to complete his revenge upon her.

"I'll not stay away, Mia," he said calmly. "Your charms have seen to that."

"No." She glanced about frantically looking for some sort of protection. Suddenly, he leaped across the overturned divan. It was not an ordinary leap of an ordinary mortal man. It was a magical flying leap of the Chameleon type. "How? How is it so?"

He reached her then and slammed her body against his. A feral witch's growl escaped her. It was one of both anger and desire. Her head swam with contradictory stimuli, for to stir up the wrath of a sorcerer was pure stupidity. But to stir his loins meant utter ecstasy.

"Your spell of Article Three Hundred Thirteen, Section *Mon-sporal*, states that, once your mortal subject has lived out a life of solitary confinement for the exact number of years — to the day — of the Article number itself, he or she will become a Chameleon apprentice."

"No," she insisted. She shook her head emphatically and flew to the wall where shelves lined its expanse from floor to ceiling. Her arm went up, and, like a magnet, it located her copy of the *Chameleon Coventry*, a holy manual of spells. It popped from the shelf and glided across the room to her. She wetted her finger and thumbed through the pages. She found what she was looking for. Her eyes quickly scanned the gold-edged page of the ancient book, and she mumbled as she speed-read it.

She spun, then, on her heel. The book tumbled through the air and crashed against a far wall. "I used the spell of Article Three Hundred *Fourteen*, not Thirteen. I still had another year to go before the clause took effect."

He slowly shook his head, almost with pity. Within a witch's blink, he was standing before her again in all his naked glory. His eyes were now a swirl of green and blue. She forced her gaze from the sight of those eyes. He was mocking her! He was laughing at her...and he was horny for her!

How stupid could she have been? How had she overlooked, or miscounted the years? Obviously, that had been why she'd suddenly felt the urge to go to Perish. It had been her last chance to avoid that particular aspect of the spell, though she'd assumed on a conscious level that she still had another year to go. As the spell's rules were written, the subject of the spell grows a temporary *trifed,* and on the anniversary, it matures. If any form of sexual contact comes between the witch and her victim, and especially once sexual consummation occurs following the hour of anniversary, the subject is made permanently immortal and becomes Chameleon. She had always thought of it as catching a disease of mixed proportions, for not all mortals desired to become immortal, magic-wielding beings.

And now she knew why he'd not allowed her to touch his ass during lovemaking, why he'd never presented his backside to her. He had had the upper hand all along, even after she'd flown the coop.

Except for the spell. If she hadn't have reversed it, he would still be imprisoned inside Perish's boundaries, because even a Chameleon could be bound by certain spells of other Chameleons.

He lifted a hand and tipped her chin up so that she had no choice but to look into them.

"Your eyes are…pink," she said with a gulp, confused, for she knew what it meant.

"Pink is the color of Chameleon love."

All Chameleon knowledge was imparted to a spell recipient. It was how he'd seemed to know the answers to everything; how, for instance, he'd known to strip his clothing at the sound of her approach to Perish. If the spell were reversed before the completion of the transformation from human to Chameleon, amnesia would take effect.

Clearly, Abraham Warwick did not have amnesia. He was now an all-knowing, almighty sorcerer — thanks to her own stupidity.

"Love?" she croaked.

"Yes," he said hoarsely, his hands rising to cup her face. He dropped his forehead to hers. "I have both loved and hated you since you arrived that day in 1692 in Perish."

Tears stung her eyes, but she refused to let them fall. His warmth engulfed her. His love suddenly overwhelmed her. "You loved me so much you threatened to burn me at the stake."

"Yes, for show."

"For show?"

He sighed and gathered her against him. "It was the town council that insisted you were a witch, and that you should be burned to death, as many others were being sentenced at that time in Salem. I had a plan. I was totally smitten with you, but I couldn't let on, or I would be imprisoned. I no longer wished to be the town's clergy, though I had already been having my doubts before you even arrived in my life. Witch or not, I had fallen madly under your spell. It had been my plan to make them all believe that I agreed and would follow through with the burning ceremony—to buy time, you see. I had intended to go to you, the very night you cast your wrath upon me, and flee with you before they could harm you. You never gave me the chance to explain. Suddenly, with one chant and one flick of your hand, I was alone...for an eternity. And I have thought of nothing else but you for the last three hundred thirteen years."

"Oh, Abe," she cried, and her arms clamped around him as she buried her face against the wall of his bare chest. "I'm so sorry, so very sorry I put you through all that maddening loneliness!"

"Shh, shh." He clutched her to him as if he feared she'd flee, as if many lifetimes of relief had just flooded his soul. "I know how you can make it up to me, love. Shh, shh."

Her tears stilled. His hardness was pressed against her abdomen, stirring the cauldron of her desire. As the fire blazed in the small hearth across the room, as the clock ticked softly, she was suddenly aware of the beat of his heart, the scent of his warm skin. How had she missed all this about him in 1692? Had she been that self-centered back then? Had she really been so cruel as to sentence him to a life of solitary confinement? Oh, how she wished she could go back and change it all. A Chameleon's life and form were all about mystical change, but that was one thing they could not do. Go back in time and alter events.

"What? What can I do, Abe? I'll do anything to make it up to you!" she cried, lifting her head so that she could look into his eyes, his heart.

The pink glow of his eyes blazed then with a swirl of blue, and his stare widened. He gaped at her for a long, eternal minute. "You already have," he finally said, his voice thick with emotion.

"I—I have?"

He whirled her around and threw a bolt of orange fire across the room. The huge, filigree-edged mirror above the mantle zipped through the space of the room and planted itself on the floor before her.

"See?" he asked softly in her ear, his hot breath sending delicious chills up her spine.

She looked at her reflection in the mirror. A ragged gasp echoed in the room. Her hand came up to slap her open mouth.

Her eyes were flaming pink! The color of love!

"It can't be," she insisted, shaking her head.

"Oh, but it can," he declared, sweeping her clothes from her in one flick of his fingers.

She swallowed audibly and studied their naked forms in the mirror. "You've become quite the warlock."

"Love cannot be forced, even by spells," he said wisely. And she knew it was true.

He swept her to the floor. The violent move jostled the end table next to the chair where she'd been relaxing. Her cup of iced tea splattered across the floor, ice cubes and all.

She cared not about the mess, and had no choice but to lay in waiting for him. She was in dire need of her daily fix.

"Be my partner, Mia."

He collapsed and covered her body with his. His mouth was all over her flesh, tearing it to wanton pieces. His sword was positioned at the apex to her soul.

"Your partner?" she panted, lifting her chin to allow him more area to feast upon her neck.

"You know what I mean," he said between nips and kisses. "Take me as your mate."

Ah, the ultimate union between Chameleons. "You want to become the Priest of the Chameleon Coven?" she asked, already feeling her honey ooze out onto the cool wood of the floor.

"Not so much that as your eternal mate. Join with me," he begged huskily. "Now."

She didn't have to ponder the request. When love was mutual between Chameleons, it was understood to unite. But with her being the High Priestess, the queen of all Chameleons, taking an eternal mate was something to mull over, to make a careful determination, for her mate would then be over the entire Coven as their king, of sorts.

"Are you prepared for the responsibility?" she asked as an electric charge moved from his mouth, where it now sucked one of her nipples into its warmth, to the ends of her claw-toes.

They both knew what was expected of them in order to complete the merging. Mutual agreement and a soulful joining.

"Yes. But only if I can have you forever..." And his mouth moved lower still. She turned then, and awed, watched in the mirror as their betrothed images bonded. A jagged neon bolt grew from her womb to connect with his scrotum. Now, all that was required was their first mutual orgasm together. He would then become her mate, the High Priest. Her husband.

Suddenly, she wanted it, wanted him, more than anything in the whole galaxy. Her breath came in short spurts. Butterflies of fire teased at her flesh as he worshiped her body. When he closed his mouth over her sex, she thought for sure she was burning at the stake.

"Abe!" she whimpered. She thrust her hips upward to meet his mouth, and he devoured her, lapping up every drop of her juice. He morphed his tongue then, adding inches to its length—and he fucked her with it, driving it into her with an animal's frenzy.

She was almost there. The orgasm surrounded her, intoxicating her with lust upon the horizon.

And he abruptly withdrew.

She gasped and looked down the length of her body at him. Was he going to start that again, that torture? "Abe?"

He grinned wolfishly at her from his place between her legs, and held up one of the elongated ice cubes from her icemaker. Then he inserted one cube into her pussy. She flinched at the cold sensation as it was sucked up inside her. He took another and repeated the process.

"Feel good?" he asked, slithering up her front side and rising gently into the air. He was now hovering over her, suspended as he looked down upon her.

"Yes…oh, yes!" she growled. Her hands went up and cupped her own tits. She pinched her nipples and a gush of cool water dripped from her pussy. "More. I want more."

He chuckled and obliged without pause. His cock was swollen and hard poised above her slit, and she wondered if he were to get anymore horny, if it would pop. He shoved two more pieces of ice into her. She stiffened at the erotic sensation of it.

But that was nothing compared to the feel of him entering her, abrading the ice against her sensitive G-spot. It melted quickly, cold trickling over warmth as it oozed from her, but the newer ones were still persevering. He drove into her, and she thought she would die by the bewitching thrill of it. His mouth covered hers in an urgent, yet gentle kiss. The floor was hard and cool at her back, and her ass abraded against it with each thrust. She spread her legs wide for him. The fervor was building.

"It is time," she said to him, and he looked down at her, his eyes a marbly mixture of blue and green, pink and, yes, even a smidgen of yellow.

"I love you, Mia," he said hoarsely, straining to hold back his release.

Her hand went up and she pressed her palm to his cheek. "And I love you, Abraham."

It was all that was needed before the finale. He gathered her to him and tossed up a hand so that they levitated in an upright position above the floor. Mia could almost touch the ceiling, but she didn't want to. She only wanted the feel of his corded muscles against her palms. She straddled his hips and rode him like a stallion. Throwing her head back, she reveled in the journey as they rose high into the Coven realm. Their mouths were melded together, and their loins connected. All was aligned correctly for their betrothal.

Then they both cried out. Their bodies sizzled together in a pink cloud of light. They twitched and seized, and the multiple orgasms went on and on.

When finally they were spent, they lost consciousness and floated back to the parlor floor.

* * * * *

"Well," Sue said blandly, her hands on her hips as she looked down at the two lovers. "I guess he *did* lay a hand on you."

Mia's eyes popped open and she looked up at an upside-down Sue. Gratefully, she and Abe had been wound in a silk covering following the ceremony, though she had no recollection of that particular ritual.

She grinned up at Sue and giggled. "Oh, yes. Many hands."

There was a deep clearing of the throat. James came into view. "You gonna help with the move?" he asked, a thick folder of signed documents from the loan closing tucked under his arm. "Or are you gonna be lazy and fuck around all night?"

"Fuck around all night," Abe offered, his voice muffled where it was tucked in the thickness of her hair. He didn't bother to lift his head and introduce himself.

Sue stifled a giggle.

"Well," James said, raising a single auburn brow, "there goes that. Gee, Sue," he said good-naturedly, slanting a look at his fiancée. "Guess we're gonna have to do all the hard work ourselves."

She nodded her agreement and added, "Yep, we'd never dream of interrupting such passion and fire."

James slipped an arm around Sue as they turned away and left the room. "Damn, that was hot," they heard him say. "Wanna go upstairs and fuck?"

"You didn't cast the horny spell on them, did you?" Abe asked, lounging now on one side, his head propped in one hand.

"Hell, no. Those two don't need it. They screw like rabbits as it is!"

The doorbell rang.

"Shit! Who could that be?"

Abe shrugged and mumbled a few words. Within a flash, they were both fully dressed. Mia went out into the foyer to answer the door. Abe propped one shoulder against the doorjamb, waiting to see who was on his wife's doorstep. Mia pulled open the heavy oak door. A cold night wind blew in.

"Trick or Treat!" two little voices chimed.

There was a long pause then Mia broke out into a rolling fit of laughter. Abe just gawked in confusion.

There, standing on her doorstep holding out bags for Halloween treats, poised a miniature witch and warlock. Mia brought herself under control, crossed to the small table in the entry where she typically tossed her keys, and opened the lone drawer.

She pulled out two bags of her favourite candy coated chocolates and offered them to Abe. "Here, drop one in each bag. I'll explain later."

The End

About the author:

Titania Ladley began her journey into reading romance at the tender age of 13. Soon, sweet romance just didn't cut it. She craved more detail, more sex, *way* more "creativity" between lovers. By her 20's, she discovered that people actually wrote what she needed to read—what she fantasized about. She then devoured the erotica genre. But, alas, restless as usual, she could no longer tolerate just *reading* about it. In her 30's, Titania couldn't suppress the need, the overwhelming drive to create her own fantasies. She had to write. So she did. Published in erotic romance novels and best-selling novellas, she just can't seem to tame her active imagination. So she writes some more...

Titania is a registered nurse, magazine freelance writer, book reviewer and has penned witty slogans. She resides in the Midwest with her very own hunky hero and three children. She enjoys reading erotic romances, walking, weightlifting, crocheting and baking fattening desserts.

Titania welcomes mail from readers. You can write to her c/o Ellora's Cave Publishing at P.O. Box 787, Hudson, Ohio 44236-0787.

Also by Titania Ladley:

Jennie in a Bottle
Moonlight Mirage
Me Tarzan, You Jewel
You've Got Irish Male: Enchanted Rogues anthology

Why an electronic book?

We live in the Information Age—an exciting time in the history of human civilization in which technology rules supreme and continues to progress in leaps and bounds every minute of every hour of every day. For a multitude of reasons, more and more avid literary fans are opting to purchase e-books instead of paperbacks. The question to those not yet initiated to the world of electronic reading is simply: *why?*

1. *Price.* An electronic title at Ellora's Cave Publishing runs anywhere from 40-75% less than the cover price of the <u>exact same title</u> in paperback format. Why? Cold mathematics. It is less expensive to publish an e-book than it is to publish a paperback, so the savings are passed along to the consumer.

2. *Space.* Running out of room to house your paperback books? That is one worry you will never have with electronic novels. For a low one-time cost, you can purchase a handheld computer designed specifically for e-reading purposes. Many e-readers are larger than the average handheld, giving you plenty of screen room. Better yet, hundreds of titles can be stored within your new library—a single microchip. (Please note that Ellora's Cave does not endorse any specific brands. You can check our website at www.ellorascave.com for customer recommendations we make available to new consumers.)

3. *Mobility.* Because your new library now consists of only a microchip, your entire cache of books can be taken with you wherever you go.

4. *Personal preferences are accounted for.* Are the words you are currently reading too small? Too large? Too...**ANNOYING**? Paperback books cannot be modified according to personal preferences, but e-books can.

5. *Innovation.* The way you read a book is not the only advancement the Information Age has gifted the literary community with. There is also the factor of what you can read. Ellora's Cave Publishing will be introducing a new line of interactive titles that are available in e-book format only.

6. *Instant gratification.* Is it the middle of the night and all the bookstores are closed? Are you tired of waiting days—sometimes weeks—for online and offline bookstores to ship the novels you bought? Ellora's Cave Publishing sells instantaneous downloads 24 hours a day, 7 days a week, 365 days a year. Our e-book delivery system is 100% automated, meaning your order is filled as soon as you pay for it.

Those are a few of the top reasons why electronic novels are displacing paperbacks for many an avid reader. As always, Ellora's Cave Publishing welcomes your questions and comments. We invite you to email us at service@ellorascave.com or write to us directly at: 1337 Commerce Drive, Suite 13, Stow OH 44224.

Discover for yourself why readers can't get enough of the multiple award-winning publisher Ellora's Cave. Whether you prefer e-books or paperbacks, be sure to visit EC on the web at www.ellorascave.com for an erotic reading experience that will leave you breathless.

WWW.ELLORASCAVE.COM

Printed in the United States
67731LVS00001B/310-333